All My Memories

Grea Warner

All My Memories
2nd Edition- 2021
Copyright © 2017 Grea Warner
All rights reserved.

ISBN: (ebook): 978-1-953335-41-8
(print) 978-1-953335-42-5

Inkspell Publishing
207 Moonglow Circle #101
Murrells Inlet, SC 29576

Edited By Yezanira Venecia
Cover art By Najla Qamber

OTHER BOOKS BY GREA WARNER

COUNTRY ROADS SERIES:

Country Roads

Almost Heaven

Take Me Home

Teardrop in My Eye

The Place I Belong

OTHER BOOKS:

Every Mile a Memory

Heads Carolina

COMING SOON:

Tails California

Whiskey Girl

GREA WARNER

DEDICATION

This prequel to the Country Roads series is dedicated to my parents who from the start have provided me with memories of unyielding love, patience, and support.

CURRENT DAY

Finn

Another one. Another text or tweet or some other electronic message. Another time someone wanted something. I'd like to ignore the chirping contraption because, in some ways, my phone is the bane of my existence. But, it's also a savior … a connector. It's, essentially, my lifeline to the crazy, super pumped-up world I always wanted but never truly envisioned would happen. So I deal with it—the beeps, the chirps, the vibrations, and the ringtones. Because, for the most part, I wouldn't want it any other way. Just occasionally, I wish I could get a break.

I looked at the screen, expecting some kind of congratulatory note from a fellow musician or another request for an appearance from my publicist. It wasn't either, though. It was Iva. She always forwarded little tidbits about the music industry, as if I didn't already know. If I did not respond, she'd send out a generic "hope all is well" message. I knew she was doing it to keep in touch and probably had the purest of intentions, but I didn't have the time. Plus, even though she's nice enough,

1

there wasn't a spark. And I'm not sure there ever will be—with her or anyone else.

Regardless, I read the message: *I heard you are in town. We should get together.*

Damn my sister and her matchmaker in-laws. They were the ones who started this whole Iva business. In a moment of lonely vulnerability, I'd let them set me up with her. But they needed to leave it alone. If I wanted Iva to know I was up North, I would have told her. I didn't need them broadcasting where I was to her.

What to do? How to respond? Should I lie and say I wasn't in town? Should I say I was extra busy during my short visit? It wasn't too far from the truth. Or, should I simply tell her it wasn't going to work out? No, I decided, I'm not good with leaving. I knew that about myself.

I contemplated my options as I stepped through the skyscraper's revolving glass door and into the bustling Lower-Manhattan business district. I had just finished discussing future projects with some of the label's head honchos. So between thinking of upcoming collaborations and trying to figure out how to deal with Iva, I didn't see it coming. I should have. There were always one or two who figured out where to position themselves to see a celebrity. And in front of a record label's building was a sure bet.

"Finn! It's Finn Murphy," the redhead screeched.

I kept my hands down, even though I wanted to cover my ears from the noise. After all, a fan was a fan, and I did appreciate all they had given me. I only wished they didn't have to do it with a sneak attack and holler at the top of their lungs.

"Hi," said her friend, a blonde. She was bubbly but, thankfully, a little more subdued. "Congrats on the CMA nominations."

"Thanks," I replied while moving my aviator sunglasses over my eyes. I didn't have in my trademark, green contact lenses that the label preferred I wear, and I didn't want to disappoint any fans with my plain gray hues. "You follow country music, I guess?"

"We both do." The redhead added to the conversation. "We go to every concert we can, especially the ones on campus."

I figured. Sorority girls. They had the screech down pat.

"That's great. That's actually how I started." I closed my eyes for the slightest of moments remembering the exhilaration of my first time on a stage. The local bars … the bad sound equipment … the lonely mic … having only friends in the audience … playing solely for tips or beer. Things had changed a lot since then, but my excitement and passion for the craft hadn't. "Sorry, girls, my ride is here."

The valet pulled up in my steely blue coupe. Perfect timing, as my ability to continue small talk was running thin. I took refuge in my car, which had been my guilty-pleasure gift to myself after winning the CMA for new artist. Throwing on my seat belt, I planned on heading straight uptown to my NYC penthouse. Located near Central Park, it was a little piece of heaven amongst the chaos and buzz of the city, which truly never seemed to sleep.

In some ways, the penthouse was the same as my main residence—a sprawling house in Nashville, Tennessee. They both were secure and contained all the newest amenities on the market. The difference was, the Nashville location had the serenity of space around it. During my wildest college-band dreams, I never could have imagined living in one of my homes, let alone, owning both.

No sooner had I started driving north, than my phone rang through the coupe's hands-free system. A quick glance at the dash told me it was my older sister. I always picked up for family. But this time, I had a bone to pick with my one and only sibling.

"Nol," I started right away. "Why did you tell Iva I was going to be in town?"

"Good grief … what a way to answer the phone,

Munch," she bounced right back.

Ah, there she went with the damn nickname. Geez, that was in grade school. I would never live it down. So what if I ate all the snacks in the house growing up? I'd been a strapping young lad and had burned off the calories with my excessive energy. She should've been glad it kept her from ruining her girly figure she was had been so concerned about then.

"Seriously, Nola."

"Finn …" Her breathy pout seemed exaggerated via the car's excellent speaker system. "I didn't tell her anything. She's Will's mom's friend. I don't even really know her."

"Well, she knows I'm here."

"Um, you're not hard to track, especially with the media surrounding the award announcements this week."

I knew it was the truth. While I liked getting to see my sister, her husband, and their kids, the real reason I was in the vicinity was to announce the CMA nominees on national television that morning. So, yeah, okay, Nola might not have been the nark. Of course, I didn't acknowledge that out loud, though.

"And, besides, is Iva that bad?" she asked.

"No," I admitted. "No, I guess not. I don't know where it's ever going to lead, though."

"Don't worry about where it's going to lead. Enjoy the company." Before I could interject, she added, "She's a nice lady."

Lady. God, using that term made me feel so old. But, I guess, maybe I was. Geez, my thirtieth birthday was right around the corner. How did that happen?

"Just because you have earned every award known to the country music world …"

"Hardly." I shook my head. I'd received some beginning ones. I had many more to tackle.

"Well, more than most. Anyway, my point is, it doesn't mean you should live the rock star lifestyle forever. Don't let what happened with Audrey mess you up from the good ones out there."

Audrey *had* messed me up, and my sister knew it. She was one of the few who actually understood to what extent. Audrey had been years ago, though. And even though she was part of my hesitancy, the job had a hand in it, too. I didn't know who wanted to be with me for *me* and not because of the fame, notoriety, or money. If I wanted to get laid, hell, sure—that was a no-brainer. I could "get some" practically whenever I wanted. But to trust someone with my heart and know they would always be there … I wasn't so sure.

"I'll call her." I found myself agreeing and then changed the subject. "So, what's up? I'm pretty sure you didn't call to talk about my love life."

"Uh, yeah. I'd prefer not to." The inflection in her voice reminded me of our teenage years, and I stifled a laugh. "You know the thing at Wyatt's school?"

"Yeah?"

Nola had texted me the night before. Her son's school, located about an hour away in their suburban New York neighborhood, wanted to raise money for one of the students who was suffering from some kind of heart disease. It seemed serious and very sad—literally heartbreaking. Nola let me know that my six-year-old chatterbox of a nephew had volunteered me to sing. Truth was, I'd do anything for the little guy. He was the coolest kid ever created. Although, his little sister, Kelsea, equaled the love in my heart, too.

I'd agreed, of course, for Wyatt and for the student who was so sick. But it made me a bit sad because I knew with Wyatt blurting out my family connection, it would change things. My sister, her husband, and the kids would no longer have total privacy in their new community. They'd be connected to me and my celebrity. While, admittedly, it had its perks, it also came with cautions and scrutiny.

"What's going on with the fundraiser?" I continued. "Did you tell them I could help?"

"Yeah. I went into the school today and talked with the people in charge. So … Finn …"

"Yeah?"

Uh-oh. Why was she hesitating? What did she get me into? I didn't want press or any meet-and-greets where people were trying to touch me in places they shouldn't. I simply wanted to sing and help the student's family.

"I met with two of the women in charge of setting up the fundraiser."

"Uh-huh." Although I loved driving, doing it during rush hour in the Big Apple demanded my full attention, and my sister was distracting me with her bizarre version of twenty questions. I gripped the leather steering wheel a little tighter and pleaded, "Nol, I'm in Manhattan traffic. What's up?"

"One of them is the technology coordinator for the school."

An instant vision of a nerdy tech girl with horned-rimmed glasses and no personality came to mind. She'd probably have a billion ideas on how to broadcast cheesy videos behind me. I hated to stereotype but, nine times out of ten, it was true.

"No hoopla videos," I admonished. "Simple, right?"

"No. That's not why I'm telling you. Her name is Lara."

Nola had paused. But had she not, I don't think I would have heard her anyway. The announcement of that name alongside the job title made my brain momentarily turn to haze, and my stomach did an immediate somersault of weird hope and shock.

"Lara Faulkner." She clinched the deal with the last name.

There had been a legitimate reason for the belly aerobics. It was Lara. Of all … Wow.

Oops, sorry, Mr. Taxi Cab Driver. I silently apologized

for the near-collision. I hadn't been paying attention. I wasn't focused on the road ... at all.

"Lara Faulkner, as in ..." I finally managed.

"Yeah, the same one."

It had been what ...? God, seven years since we had last spoken or seen one another. All my memories of her and our more innocent, collegiate days in West Virginia came rushing back—not that they were ever too far. And I wondered if Lara was thinking of back then, too.

EIGHT YEARS BEFORE …

SPRING SEMESTER

CHAPTER ONE

Finn

"Sam!" I smacked the back of my friend's head from my seat behind his driver's one. "Why is this girl at the library? No one goes to the library. It's smelly and musty and ... no one goes to the library. Plus, it's Friday night."

"Finn Murphy," his girlfriend/ball and chain/pain in the ass scolded me. "You be quiet. Lara is my friend. You'll like her. Just flash those pearly whites and sing her a tune." She had the nerve to wink at me.

I only tolerated Olivia because of Sam, and my "pearly whites" were biting at the chance to tell her off. If Lara was a friend of Olivia's, she already had one strike against her. And whether *she* knew it or not, I knew they were setting us up. Sam did it for Olivia but probably also for himself so he wouldn't have a third wheel around. I was open to it, though. While I didn't really have a problem meeting girls, the quality around campus seemed a little flimsy. All the ones I'd met so far were sorority flakes. But just like Olivia, Lara wasn't in a chapter. So maybe she would be different. And maybe she liked country music and would like our mini-band. I mean, it *could* happen.

Since I knew nothing about her, though, the verdict was definitely still out.

The co-ed in question was standing on the steps of the library as our car pulled up. She looked at her watch, toward us in the car, and then once more back and forth. I glanced at my phone. We were a few minutes late but not worthy of the whole look-up-and-down-at-the-time thing. The show couldn't start until I arrived, anyhow.

The time issue was quickly put to rest, though, as I got a better look at Olivia's friend. She had long, platinum hair—blonde like a Barbie doll's. Wearing jean shorts and a red T, her figure wasn't super skinny, but she also didn't appear to have the beer gut some of the other girls did. And her eyes were a mystical turquoise shade, like one of the nearby rivers on a sunny day.

Well, so far, so good, I thought. Taking a swig of my beer, I watched as she opened the back door. I made a spot for her by scooting closer to Bryan and patting the empty seat to the left of me.

"I'm so ready!" This new addition to our carpool surprised me with her enthusiastic entrance, and I felt her leg momentarily graze mine. "So which one of you is the singer?"

"I am." I reversed the ball cap on my short brown locks so I could see more of her and less of the hat rim. "He's added baggage." I punched my friend and guitarist, Bryan, in the arm.

"Yeah, right." Bryan shook his head, causing his tiny black curls to slightly bounce.

"Liv, do the introductions," Sam directed as he started driving once again.

"I'm Olivia." Olivia thought she was being cute or something, as she looked back and waved to us. She wasn't.

The newbie next to me, however, thought Olivia was funny. Oh boy. Strike two.

"Lara, Finn, Bryan." Olivia pointed to each of us in a

row as she said our names.

"Nice to meet you." Lara inched her leg away from me as if repulsed, but she sounded nice and genuine. "So what songs are you going to sing?"

"Some R.E.M., Springsteen, James Taylor. But we mostly do country covers," I answered.

"Great. That's what I grew up on. I remember when my brother first sang 'Tractor's Sexy.' I laughed my head off thinking there was no way that song was legit. And, if it was, who would listen to it? Then, I became a fan."

"Yeah, that's Kenny. We do a lot of Toby—'Whiskey Girl?'" I threw out a song title.

"Ragged-on-the-edges girl," she recited part of the lyrics, making me think maybe I was too hasty with the last strike.

Bryan put on a pair of cheap, non-prescription specs and turned his head in a couple of different directions. "So, what do you think?" he asked the new passenger. "We're thinking one of us should add glasses to break up the look. We picked these up at a thrift shop." He handed them to me.

When I tried them on, Lara had an answer I was not expecting. "Well, you ..." she said, nodding at Bryan, "they look good on. You"—she directed her glance at me—"not so much."

"Ha!" Bryan openly laughed.

"You might do better putting on a cowboy hat, too, instead of a ball cap. You look like a cancer patient instead of a country singer," she added.

Geez! Well, that was a little rude or forward or ... Oh, yeah, she was Olivia's friend. Well, library girl just lost the point she had earned back.

"Bro, you look fine in the baseball hat," Sam chimed in from the driver's seat.

"Really?" I didn't want to let it show, but I was seriously taken aback. I'd never tell someone they looked like a cancer patient or make any kind of derogatory comment about their appearance—at least not to their face.

"Now, who are you going to trust?" the pretty but abrupt blonde continued. "Someone who is your friend and is obligated to tell you that you look good, or someone who you don't know and has no reason to lie to you?"

"You want some of my beer?" I asked, not knowing what else to say.

This girl had been talking a mile a minute since she'd first entered the car. She either needed a beer or she'd already had one too many. I tipped my bottle toward her.

"What? I'm not good enough to have my own?" she questioned.

Oh, geez. How long was this car ride? "I'd get you one, but they're in the trunk right now." Once again, I tried to be gentlemanly and hand her my beer.

"No. I don't know you well enough to share a drink with you."

Fine. It meant more alcohol for me. And I felt like I was really going to need it with how the evening had begun.

I brought the bottle up to my lips before saying, "Then tell us something about yourself."

She let out a long, breathy sigh, and I wondered whether it was because of the subject or about me. "Well, let's see, you know where I go to school."

"Major?" Bryan, thank God, tagged in on the conversation once again.

"Computer Science."

"That's what my girlfriend is into, too," my solo bandmate offered.

"Oh, does she go to school here?"

"No. Community college." He shrugged. "Well, there should definitely be jobs available in that field. Everything is electronic. Unless the computers take the jobs," he joked, but it probably wasn't too far from the truth.

"I simply want a job. I'll move anywhere. Totally not

homebound." There seemed to be a flash of dark blue in her eyes instead of the pure turquoise, and it made me wonder about the reason. "I'd love to be near a big city. Feel the rush … the pace. Not moseying along in the local mall."

The girl confused the heck out of me. It was as if we were on a seesaw. The scorekeeper was going to need a rest. Maybe it would come down to a judge's decision at the end of the night.

"Yeah, me, too," I spoke. "Not my whole life, though. It's a young person's world. What age do you think suburbia hits?"

"Thirty-five?" she ventured, and I couldn't help but think that sounded so ancient.

"Lara, how come we haven't seen you around campus before?" I questioned, knowing she was a junior just like the rest of us in the car and the liberal arts college's population wasn't huge.

"I only transferred in last year and have been trying to make up credits. But I'm still gonna be a whole semester behind on graduation." Her voice grew softer as she shifted her eyes downward.

"Well, that's part of it." Olivia laughed from her broomstick in the front seat. "She's also part tech worm, part vampire. She can't get off her computer long enough to have a social life."

It was quite noticeable by the piercing of Lara's eyes that she didn't care for her friend's comment. So, in consolation, I tilted my beer toward her again. And, that time, she took it. It was a solid swig, but she obviously didn't like the taste. Her nose scrunched up, and she handed the bottle right back.

"Well, no matter, it's nice you're out with us tonight," I offered in more of an effort to counteract Olivia's poor social graces than anything else.

Lara did a quick blink-and-you'd-miss-it smile and said, "Thanks," as we pulled up to the venue.

I started setting up everything for the night's performance. Sam and Bryan helped, too. Olivia and Lara had their heads bundled together in girl talk. But the whole night, no matter how many times I tried to get Miss Faulkner's attention from the stage, she didn't once look at me. She didn't even dance for long. She might as well have stayed in the library on her laptop or whatever.

I decided the ruling was a draw. She obviously wasn't into me, and I didn't have the patience for a stuck-up, too-good-for-music princess. I purposefully switched seats with Olivia for the ride back. And when the night ended, I wished her well, like any other casual acquaintance I thought I would never see again.

Lara

I try. I do. I try to go out, and I try to act normal. I try to do the things that girls my age like to do. Sometimes I'm all for it, but sometimes it takes a whole lot of self-motivating talks to get me to join in.

Going to see Sam's friend play at the town bar was a mix of both. Feeling exhilarated about completing a class assignment I had struggled with, I wanted to relax and have fun. Getting to know new people was not a strength of mine, though. And meeting boys my age? That was the worst.

Despite maybe talking more than usual in the car and with sarcasm new people didn't understand, I thought I did pretty well. But then came the bar ... and I couldn't help myself. I turned into that other Lara—the Lara I really wished could have remained in Pennsylvania when I had transferred schools. I knew how I came across. I was like an old fuddy-duddy—the ruin-the-fun-for-everyone gal.

It started with the dancing. I don't know why people try to get me to dance. Just because they liked it, didn't mean I did.

"C'mon, it's a fast dance!" Olivia screamed over the sound of Bryan's guitar. "Anything goes."

"Dance with Sam," I tried to encourage as a reply.

"Eh." She flung her hand in the air. "He's a lost cause. He's found the pool table, and I'm lucky he at least accommodates me with the slow dances. C'mon …" she urged again with a tug of my arm.

"I really don't want—"

It didn't matter what I wanted. Thanks to Olivia, I found myself on the dance floor. I tried to find some kind of rhythm, but my hips only managed to sway left to right and my arms seemed to just be able to raise chest height, as if I were in defense mode ready for a blow. Olivia was next to me smiling like a nutball having the time of her life, and strangers were all around, occasionally bumping into me. I felt so embarrassingly awkward. It was as if all the spotlights were on me and not the stage where that Finn guy was singing. I didn't dare look in his direction. I couldn't even imagine what he was thinking.

After a song and a half, I made the excuse to use the restroom. Staying there as long as I could, I then reentered the main room, bought a sparkling water, and claimed a seat near the wall. Olivia didn't bother me to dance again. It was a slow song when I returned, anyway. So Sam was there. And on the faster songs, she had already drank enough to not really care who was dancing with her.

Then there was that … the drinking. I should have known when they had already started partaking in the car that it was going to be that kind of night. I had come up with excuses not to drink when Finn offered to share his beer. Olivia's belittling comment had made me give in, though, and with such a low tolerance, those couple of sips had given me an instant, extremely rare buzz.

That had been enough alcohol for me. But obviously not for the rest of them. With the exception of designated driver Sam, everyone switched over to rum concoctions after the music had started. Watching them and how they acted made me think … and remember … and worry. I didn't have fun. I didn't have fun at all.

CHAPTER TWO

Finn

I was in the quad with a bunch of my buddies when I saw Lara a few days later. Even though the date set-up hadn't panned out, I could still be nice. I mean, she wasn't awful … just not for me. So, I nodded in her direction and gave a slight wave. I know she had to have seen me—she was walking by herself only a few yards away. But nothing. Not a smile. Not a wave back. Nothing. She just continued on.

"Well, that was a blow-off." My friend mockingly punched me in the side, and the rest of my supposed pals laughed with robust.

"Ha. Ha," I replied while watching Lara turn her head for the slightest of seconds back in our direction. "So much for trying to be a nice guy. Anyway …" I could blow her off, too. "I'm meeting Sam at the caf. Anyone coming?"

I knew they weren't, though. They all had classes to attend. I had an earlier lunch break. So did Sam … and not Olivia—a rare time when I saw my friend without his other half. Miracle of miracles.

I made my way down the brick walkway, through the parking lot, and into the cafeteria. Sam was already in line, so I grabbed a tray and snuck in beside him. We then found a table near the center of the room, close to the salad bar. That was my usual lunch go-to. Although, one would hardly consider what I ate as a salad. Red potatoes, tortilla chips, chickpeas, cheese, and ranch dressing landed in my bowl. I did also throw in a sprig of lettuce to make it seem legit.

"Another Murphy masterpiece," Sam noted my food choice as I sat.

"What are you having today? Toasted O's or Raisin Bran?" I questioned Sam's daily cereal lunch.

"Hittin' it wild—going marshmallows." He smiled and scooped into the milk and cereal.

I barely had my fork to my lips when I said, "Geez, all of a sudden that girl is everywhere."

"What girl? Who?" Sam turned his neck to scan the area.

"Lara—that girl you tried to set me up with on Friday." I titled my chin in the direction where she sat. She was way in the corner of the room against the wall of windows. Next to her was a blond guy I had seen around campus but didn't know. They seemed to be looking at a laptop very intensely.

"Hey, dude, for one thing, it wasn't me who set you up."

"Yeah." I rolled my eyes—it was such a natural reaction when thinking of Olivia. I wondered if Sam ever noticed. "Well, whoever did … let's not try that one again. What's her story, anyway? I definitely got the cold-shoulder earlier. Is it because she is with that guy? Why would Olivia try to—"

"Liv doesn't think it's anything really serious with Oystein." He revealed the blond guy's name … a strange one at that. "Plus, he is graduating next week. I don't know what she was thinking setting you two up, though. Just because we're friends and she's friends with Liv, doesn't mean—"

"No kidding."

"She is a nice girl, though. Just quiet. Actually, I don't know how her and Liv are friends."

Their friendship did seem a little odd. But sometimes opposites attract. It wasn't my concern, though. I had better things on my mind.

"Still, no more setups." I pointed my finger at my friend. "Let's just have fun until break."

Lara

"So … you've seen Finn?" Olivia slowly opened the towering, wooden doors, as old as they were heavy.

"Huh? Finn?" I asked, trying to understand what she was talking about. My mind was still on the extensive assignment the professor had given as class ended. "What?"

"Have you seen him since the bar gig? He—"

"Oh, the music guy … the singer. No. Why would I have seen him?" We started making our way toward the main part of campus via the uneven walkway.

"I uh—"

"Oh, yeah," I acknowledged with fresh recollection. "I did. He waved. But I kind of only saw him at the last minute, and I didn't really think he was waving at me."

Why would he? He was with a bunch of frat boys, and they had that top-dog presence about them. It was like high school all over again. And I hated high school.

"By the time I realized, he had already turned." I recalled his action as well as my internal grimace, seeing him and his friends laughing. "Why?"

"He's good-looking. Don't ya think? Those gray eyes with the brown hair, the musician thing …" She clicked her tongue a few times.

"Yeah, but, Olivia!" I admonished.

Geez, she always acted as though she was Sam's conjoined twin … hardly ever apart. Yet there she was, fawning over one of his best friends? I knew some girls were like that, but I didn't expect it from her. I thought I knew her.

We had been friends for the second half of the scholastic year, having met in a sociology class. Needing a partner for one of the activities, she approached me, and I was appreciative, normally keeping to myself. Her straightforwardness and outgoing personality helped me branch out a little, and I think my rational outlook helped her, too. But, sometimes, I also believed I was her personal psychology project. Or maybe that was just friendship.

"What?" She played my question about her and Finn extremely innocently—not a typical Olivia trait.

"Are you and Sam … I mean, are you thinking of going for Finn?"

She let out what I was guessing was an exasperated breath. Although, my friend had so many sighs, I couldn't decipher their different meanings half the time. "I—Geez, Lara, no." With that, she started off with a practical sprint to … "Sam!" who was standing near the computer lab doors.

Sam's presence most definitely put an end to our conversation, and I was fine with it. I certainly didn't need to know Olivia's intentions. Besides, Oystein was walking toward me, and I *did* want to find out about him.

"Lara, you are looking beautiful." He always complimented me no matter my disposition or appearance. And the way he said it in his Norwegian accent was so endearing.

"Thank you."

"Ah! You believe me this time." His smile seemed to light up his pale blue eyes even more.

"No," I denied and then admitted, "I just knew saying that would make you happy." Taking a compliment was most definitely not one of my strengths.

When he shook his head, I couldn't help but wonder if that was an American trait he had picked up on. "Nei, but the final grade on my project did."

"Yeah?" It was why I was anxious to see him. I had helped him with most of the technology side.

"Ninety-eight percent."

"That's great!"

"Thanks to you."

"You're welcome. It was fun. I liked it. You deserve that grade."

"*You* deserve to be happy." He nodded. "Ja, even if not with me."

Oystein was a great guy, and I could see falling for him if given the time. But he was returning back to his country where an executive position in his family business awaited. And I wasn't ready. I just wasn't. I didn't know when I would be, but having kissed Oystein before, I felt like it could be a possibility again with someone in the future. Maybe.

Right then, though, all I wanted to do was concentrate on making it to break. It would be my second year working at a camp for the summer. As a counselor, I taught the young kids some of the newest technology. The best part, though? It was a stay-over camp away from home. That meant—besides a couple days before school resumed—I didn't have to go back home to rural Western Pennsylvania ... and that fact could not have made me any happier.

FALL SEMESTER

CHAPTER THREE

Finn

"Vern!"

There were only a couple of us gathered in the frat living room, but regardless of the number, if our brother Vern walked in, it was almost obligatory to yell out his name as if he was Norm on the old sitcom *Cheers*. How or when it started, I didn't know. But, admittedly, it was fun.

"Hey, what's up?" Kip asked Vern as I went back to writing the lyrics in front of me. "You look like—"

"I just helped my dad with a tow." Vern was a local boy, who lived off-campus and helped with his dad's garage as often as he could.

"Was there a hot, stranded girl on the side of the road?" another of our frat brothers asked. "Or—"

"It was Sam."

It wasn't just that he said my best friend's name, but it was in the slow, almost eerie inflection in which he said it that made me look up. All cars weren't towed because of breakdowns. A lot of times they—

"It seemed pretty bad." Vern was looking at me. "They hit a tree ... front end was smashed in, wheel was bent, couldn't steer …"

"Where's he at? Is he all right?" I stood while asking the flurry of questions bombarding my brain. "What do you know?"

My roommate hadn't spent the night. He had been at Olivia's as he was most of the time. So I had no idea where he would have been driving to or *any* of his plans. for the day.

"They're at General. It was him and Olivia and a girl named Lara. It happened near Cygnus Field."

"Yeah, what else? How are they?" My feet were jittering like I was tapping out the fastest beat possible.

"I don't know," Vern answered plainly, but I could tell he was concerned and the next fact told me why. "We were there after the ambulance."

"You don't know anything else?" Kip asked.

"No. Sorry." Vern looked from me to the others. "Thought I'd come and tell y'all in person. I gotta get back to my dad," he concluded with a sad look downward before taking off again.

The rest of us immediately got online to find out if there was any news of the accident. When our efforts unfortunately provided zero results, I decided to take matters into my own hands. "I'm gonna go to the hospital. I'll let you guys know what's going on."

It wasn't doing me any good staying at the frat house and replaying Vern's grim words. The more I thought, the more I worried and the worse the imaginary images became. Sam was my best friend. We had met freshman year, pledged together, and had been roomies ever since. We had always been there for each other, and a trip to the hospital was not going to be any different.

***

Not seeing Sam's parents when I arrived nor having their number, I ended up fibbing to the workers at the hospital's main desk. I told them that Sam and I were brothers. Fraternity should count, right? The hospital staff informed me that the accident had knocked him momentarily unconscious, he suffered a concussion, and he also had a broken arm. Olivia had fractured her left foot and there was something wrong with her breathing. Their injuries meant they were both going to have to stay at least overnight. Lara, in contrast, seemed to have fared a lot better with just a couple of banged-up knees. Relieved that my friend and the girls were better than I feared, I followed the nurse's directions to Olivia's room since Sam was getting some sort of treatment.

It was Lara's voice I heard when I walked in. "Sure, Liv. Sure. I can do it. It doesn't matter." Standing at Olivia's bedside, the blonde jumped a little when I cleared my throat to announce my entrance. "Oh, hi." She acknowledged my presence after turning in my direction.

"Hi," I echoed and wondered if her tone of indifference was part of the stand-offish attitude she exuded in the spring. "How you doing?"

"Better than Liv." Her words, although spoken rather plainly, at least provided some much-needed lightheartedness.

"What are *you* doing here?" Olivia's voice was uncommonly quiet and staggered, yet packed a punch with her emphasis.

"What do you think, Olivia?" I couldn't help being just as snippy back, even though I should have considered what she and the other two were going through. "We heard about the accident and I—"

"On campus? Everyone knows?" Because that should be Olivia's first concern.

I rolled my eyes. "No, just a few of us at the house," I forged on. "What happened?"

"A deer. It jumped right out in front of us. I'm sure it's not hurt, though. It's probably as safe and as lucky as Lara is."

"Yeah, right, that's me … lucky," the platinum blonde responded with undeniable sarcasm.

I ignored her seemingly loaded comment and directed my question to Olivia. "They're keeping you and Sam, huh?"

"Yeah. Overnight at least. Sam's folks are on their way here."

"I figured." I knew Sam's family didn't live too far away. Olivia's family, though, lived somewhere out of state and were hardly ever mentioned. And, not that it mattered, but I didn't have a clue about Lara's.

"Lara is gonna check on the cats at my place." The sociology major had a number of felines at her off-campus apartment.

"I just gotta find a way to get there. I'm assuming the ambulance that got everyone here isn't an option." Lara's tease was deadpan.

"Neither is the car." Olivia grumbled.

"I can take you," I offered to library girl. "It doesn't seem like I am going to see Sam, and if his parents are coming, he'll have them. I might as well head back." I didn't get an answer from Lara, though, so I tried again. "So, yeah? You want a ride?"

There was another slight pause before her reply. "You don't have to do that. I can call a taxi or something."

"Lara!" Olivia's screech had her coughing and in noticeable discomfort. "He's going back to campus anyway."

Lara seemed to be studying me with those turquoise eyes of hers when a nurse walked in and ushered us out the door because we were supposedly agitating Olivia. I wanted to say, Olivia agitated herself … as she agitated the rest of the world. Reminding myself to be kind, though, I refrained.

"Are you free to go, then? All checked out?" I asked once Lara and I were in the lobby.

"Yeah. The hospital cleared me, and I answered the

cop's questions." My shock must have shown more than I realized because she added, "Just an accident report. It's not like they are hunting down the deer. Are you sure it won't be a bother ... driving me back?"

The girl swiveled from sassy and sarcastic to innocent and sweet almost in the same breath. Admittedly, it fascinated me. I couldn't quite put my finger on it. But I was beginning to think she wasn't doing it maliciously or because she was deranged in any sense. She ... she ... I just didn't know.

Mistaking my hesitation, she continued, "Oh, never mind. I'll figure it out myself. I always do." She adjusted her brown laptop bag on her shoulder and started to walk off.

Or maybe I was right with my original diagnosis months before—she was stuck up. "Yeah, I guess a Jeep Wrangler's not good enough for you."

She, once again, turned toward me. "You have a Jeep?" Her eyes grew in size in the most positive way.

"Uh, yeah." I could have, should have, simply stood there and let her say the next thing. I should have made her feel awkward because, after all, I was the one offering to do her a favor and she was the one being all weird about it. But I couldn't. It was the courteous Southern boy in me. "C'mon, Lara, I'm a good driver. Better than Sam." I smiled to let her know I was teasing, and she actually smiled back.

"Okay, thanks. If you're sure. And, seriously, anyone is better than Sam," she played along. "So that's not saying much." Again, she was sweet and sassy and ... confusing.

Without any further debate, we started walking toward the exit in sync. That's when I heard her stomach growl. Being a few inches or so shorter than I was, she looked up at me with obvious embarrassment.

"Tell me that sound is from hunger and not that you are going to upchuck or anything. I don't want to have to wash and vacuum the seats."

"Finn Murphy!" She smacked me straight on my bicep.

It took me by surprise—the sudden action, the force of the blow, and the fact that she even remembered my name. I stumbled on one foot. "Ouch. You've got a mean right hook."

"Sorry," she immediately apologized. "Bad habit."

With the Jeep a few steps away, I debated about opening the door for her. No. No, I told myself. This wasn't a date. Geez. God. She … no.

"C'mon," I said, getting into the car.

Once we were in and started on our way a little bit, I heard her tummy rumble again. "Here." I picked up my phone, pressed the contact number, and handed it to Lara. "Order a large. I'm feeling mushrooms and sausage but get whatever you want on your half. Do you know Olivia's address? Have it delivered."

She shook her head as if startled. "I do but—Oh, uh, hi." She switched from speaking with me to the person on the other end of the phone at Pizza Pit Stop.

"A large with mushrooms and sausage …" I prompted.

She repeated my words and then said, "The other half … just plain, I guess."

Plain. Hmmm. Nope. Not plain at all. But I didn't know what type of pizza would best describe Lara Faulkner. Maybe one where the sauce was on top of the cheese because she was so darn confusing.

When she got off the phone, she said to me, "I don't have any money."

"I didn't ask you for any. My treat. Anything so your stomach quits distracting me. It doesn't even have a good tempo."

She laughed quickly. And I did, too. It was a nice change and feeling.

"So," I asked, wanting to keep our conversation going and light. "Where were you going when Bambi gave you the little detour?"

"Bambi." She tilted her head back to the headrest and

let out a sigh. "Oh, geez, like I don't already feel bad enough."

When she didn't offer any more, I bit, "Why? It sounds like the deer is fine, and you weren't driving the car."

"No, but I'm the whole reason we were in the car in the first place." She paused again. It didn't seem as if it was her natural inclination to give out information. When I made a point of looking her direction, though, she continued, "My laptop … it was freaking out. Since it is under warranty, I thought I should take it to the store. And, well, I don't have a car, and Olivia offered."

"She offered Sam," I corrected, very well knowing how the couple worked.

"Well, yeah."

"Can't do anything apart, those two." I partially grumbled.

Lara looked at me, scrunched her eyes as if in an internal debate, and then said, "Siamese."

Her sarcasm was priceless. She totally got Sam and Olivia. I was glad I wasn't drinking anything because I surely would have spewed liquid out from laughing so hard.

"Did you get your computer fixed?" I refocused, looking toward her bag.

"Yeah. That's the worst part. It was so easy. I could have done it over the phone."

"Well, that's good."

"But now they're in the hospital." Her voice dropped to a more sullen tone. "The car is a mess, the cats … I feel so bad. It's my fault. I, like, owe him a new car, and I can't do that."

"Nope. Unless you're some kind of undercover celeb, you can't go buying people cars," I teased.

"If only." She shook her head, the blonde hair all bundled up in a bun. "I can't even buy pizza with my student loans."

"The car will be fine. Sam's family will have it covered.

And no one was seriously hurt. That's really what is important."

"Thanks." She seemed genuinely grateful for my words. "The least I can do is look after the cats."

"You're a rock star for doing that."

"You're not a cat fan, either?" she asked.

"Not at all," I acknowledged. "Well, except for the Bengals."

"What?"

"The football team." I smiled at my own little joke about the team I had grown up supporting.

"Whatever," she replied, but I could tell she thought it was a little bit funny.

During the rest of the ride and then while feasting on pizza, we bonded a little more over how suckered Sam was by Olivia. Plus, I found myself telling her about my music—about booking gigs and the jittery excitement I had felt the first time I sang an original piece in public in Louisville.

"That's where you're from?" she asked while ripping off another part of her second piece of pizza. It seemed she was a pull-apart-and-eat pizza-eater, rather than a holding-the-entire-piece type.

"Yeah," I answered the hometown question and threw it back to her. "How about you?"

"Uh, my family moved around a lot for a while, but we've been near Pittsburgh for quite a few years now."

"Because of your dad?"

"Huh?" Her head shot back and she looked almost in pain.

"His job? I have tons of friends who have had to move all over because of job promotions their dads have gotten." Then I realized I was being sexist. "Sorry, your mom's? Does your mom—"

"She's a nurse in the ER."

"Well, I'm sure she had a lot to relate to when you told her what happened."

"What happened?" She seemed confused.

"Today? Your accident?" I finished my second piece of pizza.

"Oh. I haven't called them yet." It was her straightforward voice. Before I could question, she jumped in with one of her own, and it was an obvious change of subject—back to me. "What do you want to do with your music? Are you looking at it as a career?"

"Yeah, you know, sell out stadiums, be on the cover of *Rolling Stone* ..." I grinned.

"So not very lofty goals?" Her slight laugh made it seem like she was maybe a little more comfortable again.

"Not at all." I chuckled back. "I do think it would be cool to work on song tracks for movies, though."

"Yeah, music definitely helps set the tone," she agreed. "I love getting lost in a movie at the theater ... or a book. Give me a good book and I'll read it in one day."

Thoughts of library girl reentered my mind, but I didn't outwardly say anything, especially since we were having a nice conversation. "Can't say I read much besides required course work and lyrics," I admitted. Then, because she had been rubbing her face practically nonstop since we entered Olivia's apartment, I noted, "No offense, but your nose is starting to look like Rudolph's."

She immediately held up her hand to her nose. "Sorry. I ... I'm pretty allergic to cats. My nose and my eyes ... and Liv doesn't seem to have any more tissues."

"Geez, why didn't you say something?" I deplored. The pesky, furry felines were crawling all over the place ... sometimes even on us.

"I ... I don't know. I had to feed them, and then there was the pizza."

"Well, everyone is fed now. We should probably get you out of here." I stood, closing and picking up the pizza box as I did. "Let's go."

Admittedly, it was a shame, though. It would have been nice to have stayed and talked a little bit longer. But, she was a nasally, red-eyed mess. So, I drove her back to her dorm, just a small hill down from mine, and said good-bye.

Lara

As it turned out, Sam's friend was a pretty nice guy. Finn was actually more than his musician, drinking, and frat boy labels. I knew I had initially stereotyped, and I shouldn't have. Because, after all, if people knew *my* hidden tags, I'm sure I wouldn't like what they'd assume, either.

I was thinking of him the morning after the accident and the fact that I was actually kind of sad that my stupid allergies had ended our time together. It was almost as if Finn and I had formed a sort of bond over the whole ordeal. I loved that his interpretation of the Olivia and Sam dynamic exactly mirrored mine. It was so nice to have that comradery with someone.

When the telephone rang, it startled me out of my thoughts. I winced in pain as I rolled over to reach for the phone on my nearby desk. It was amazing how I forgot about the bruising on my knees until they touched something, and then … youch!

I looked at the caller ID as I sat more definitively in bed. Not recognizing the number, I answered it with some caution. "Hello?"

"Hey, uh, Lara?"

"Yeah?" Still no idea.

"It's Finn."

"Finn," I echoed.

"Murphy."

He supplied his last name as clarification, but that wasn't the reason I had repeated it. I just wasn't expecting him. *And* it was weird that I had been thinking of Finn when he called.

"Yeah, yeah," I confirmed. "I didn't know you had my

number." I very rarely gave it out, and surely I would have remembered giving it to him.

"Sam gave it to me. I just talked with him. They're being released. So they wanted me to tell you there's no need to feed the cats today."

"Oh, well that's good news."

"That they're being released or that your nose isn't going to be put through a torture chamber again?"

I burst out a legitimate laugh. "I guess both," I admitted, thinking how ridiculous I must have looked. A day later, my nose was still a little raw, but at least it didn't itch anymore. "Hey, thanks for helping out yesterday, especially since—"

I didn't get to say that I knew I was kind of bitchy at the hospital because my thank you was halted by singing. The sound wasn't coming from any kind of speaker system. It was actual voices from across the phone line.

"Happy birthday to you, happy birthday to you, happy birthday—"

"Yeah, yeah, thanks. I'm on the phone." That was Finn.

It was his birthday? Oh. I was going to acknowledge it when I heard another male voice from Finn's side of the phone.

"Cake, brother. Let's eat cake!" and then a cake chant started.

"Hey, Lara, I gotta go," the obvious birthday boy said. "They won't stop until I do."

"Happy birthday, I guess, right?" I replied.

"Yep. Thanks. Talk later."

He hung up. And my first thought was, yeah, it would be nice to talk later. It was nice to have a new friend.

CHAPTER FOUR

Lara

"I can't believe this is all happening to me. How am I supposed to ... What is that look for?"

I hadn't realized I was giving out any kind of expression until Olivia called me on it. Although when she did, I had a pretty good idea what it must have looked like. We were in the college bookstore— where we always bought more garments and candy than actual books for school, since we found those secondhand or online much cheaper. Olivia had started complaining in the adjacent coffee shop and had not stopped.

"Olivia, everyone is fine. That's what's important." When the words emerged from my mouth, it felt like they came from somewhere or some*one* else. That's when I remembered Finn telling me something very similar on the ride back from the hospital. "It's true," I said aloud but kind of meant it for myself.

"I know." She wobbled on her injured foot to the wall where some of the drugstore-like items were located. "Everything is still awful, though." She paused but only for a second. "Were you scared?"

"More after it all happened," I admitted, thinking of seeing my friends hurt at the accident site. "I didn't see the deer or what was going on until we hit … until the impact with the tree. You guys saw it. So that part wasn't bad for me."

"Sam had a nightmare about it last night. He's sensitive like that." She shook her head. "*My* nightmare is not having a car."

That time I really had to focus on not rolling my eyes. There she went again with overdramatizing rather than prioritizing. Everyone … was … fine. Plus, the car wasn't even hers. It was Sam's.

"What's happening with that?"

I tried to see her side of living just off campus and being used to commuting via car. Even though the walk was normally very doable, it had become quite burdensome with her injury. Still, there were options, and it most certainly did not qualify as a "nightmare." I knew about nightmares.

"Vern's dad said it has to be junked. He's hooking Sam up with a deal on another car. It's pretty much a piece of crap and it still costs too much, especially with some medical bills, too."

We plopped our items on the counter for the cashier. Mine … dark chocolate. Hers … ibuprofen and tampons.

"Always glad when my monthly visitor arrives," she explained the last item. "Don't want any little diaper-changers appearing."

After a momentary shutting of my eyes, I returned back to the real conversation. "Can't insurance help with the car or—?" I didn't know how car and health insurance worked. I was on my parents', and they took care of it.

"Not much. Can't really get money from the tree." She grumbled while accepting the bagged items from the clerk. As I thought it was *me* she should be getting money from—it was my fault the accident happened in the first place—she continued, "The guys are helping, though." On my furrowed brows, she explained, "The frat is having a car wash. I know … ironic. Then, right after, there will be a pay-for party at the house. All proceeds go to the Sam's Sucky Car Fund."

"Oh. I didn't know about that. When is it?"

"This weekend. Finn's kind of organizing it. Hey, can I have a piece of that … just a sliver? I could really use some chocolate."

As we exited the store, I split the bar in half. She tried to deny accepting the equal portion but gave in almost just as immediately. I had expected it. It was why I bought the bigger bar in the first place.

"It's the least I can do," I said, but I was also thinking of another way to help.

When Olivia and I parted ways for our individual classes, I found Finn's contact info under the recent calls to my phone. I sat on a bench in the quad and scripted out a text to send. It was my absolute preferred method of communication. *Liv said you guys were raising $$ for Sam. How can I help?*

As I started making my way toward my class, the unexpected sound made me jump. I pulled my cell back out from my laptop case to identify the culprit of the noise. It wasn't a text but an actual phone call from the number I recognized as Finn's. Of course he was a "talk" person. He was outgoing—his number of friends and stage presence told me that.

"Hello?" I answered, recognizing I needed to since I was the one who initiated the correspondence in the first place.

"Hey, got your text." His voice came through my phone. "Thought it would be easier to just call."

"Uh, yeah. I'm on my way to class." I adjusted the falling strap on my shoulder while still trying to hold on to the phone.

"All right. Quick then. You want to help with the thing for Sam?"

"Yeah, if you think I can."

"Absolutely. We can use all the help we can get."

"So … what?" I questioned.

"How are you with washing cars?"

"Can't be too hard, right?" It wasn't like I owned one or had a reason to wash one before.

"Easier than Econ," he grunted. "I'll sign you up, then?"

"Yeah, okay. Who will be there?"

"Some of the guys and their girlfriends. And, of course, I'll be around."

"Okay." Admittedly, knowing he would be there—someone I kind of knew—put me a little more at ease, especially when the event was at a frat house. "What else, though?" I continued. "I mean, I really want to help since I was the whole rea—"

"We're going to have a cat-grooming station, too," he interjected with enthusiasm. "I'll put you in charge. Seems like your wheelhouse."

The laughter that burst from my mouth shocked both me and the couple of fellow students who were exiting the room as I was entering. "No." I quickly reigned my voice back in. Although, internally, I was still laughing. "Don't think that would be the best—" As I started to sit, an idea came to me. "How about posters to get the word out? I can make those and put them up."

"Yeah, perfect," he immediately agreed. "Can I send you the info I already put on social media?"

"Sure. Yep. Sure." It felt good to actually be doing something to help.

"Thanks, Lara. I'll forward it to you in a few."

"Okay. Class is ready to start, but I'll get on it later and send you anything before I print."

"I'm sure it will be fine. Guess I will see you on Saturday, then."

Finn

Thanks to awesome September weather, a college that supported its own, and the posts, the turnout for the car wash was amazing. There were so many cars that we set up two washing stations. As the organizer, I was running in between there and the house making sure the others were getting the kegs, food, and anything else set for the party afterward.

"Finn, you wanna take my place so I can go get the wood from my dad?" Vern asked when I joined the car-washing group a good way into the two-hour event.

"Yeah, sure," I agreed. "Can't have a bonfire without the logs. Thank your dad for the donation."

"Sure thing. Be back in a jiffy."

Since Kip was squirting off the steel-gray AWD, I turned to Lara, who was standing with one of the towels in her hand. "So, what's my job here, Faulkner?" I questioned.

"I don't know. What's your wheelhouse?" When I smiled at her snarky comment—a sure response to mine earlier in the week—she continued, "Maybe you ought to speed-dial to get pizza for the waiting customers."

"Ha! Already done for the party after."

"So impressive," she mocked.

"How are you? Haven't seen you since—"

"I'm fine. As soon as I got away from the scent o—"

"No, I figured that," I corrected. "What about your legs or knees or whatever?"

"Oh, much better." She seemed shocked but grateful for my question before adding, "Sam and Liv had—have—it so much worse."

"Yeah, but you were in that car, too." I had a feeling that was being forgotten, and it shouldn't have been. "Just checking."

"Thank—"

"Hey," Kip interjected. "Who is drying this car off?"

I grabbed a towel and assisted Lara in drying the car. I was impressed with her mastery at detail—she didn't forget the wheels, headlights … anything. In turn, I got to the top of the automobile because I was a bit taller.

We had a few more cars like that, and then, since the time was winding down and dusk was setting in, fewer cars arrived and a quick bit of shenanigans occurred. Sponges were tossed, rags were whipped, and hoses were sprayed at one another. When I saw smirks from a few of my brothers and looked in the direction they were, I spotted the cause—Lara and her white T-shirt.

"Uh, Lara?" I walked over to her.

"Yeah?"

I pointed my index finger toward her shirt and she immediately crossed her arms in front of her bosom. Well, not exactly that. She *was* wearing a bra, but we could tell every definition of it—the straps, the lines, the spots where it met her skin.

"Oh my God." She seemed temporarily frozen in embarrassment, but then looked at the others and back to me. "I'm … I'm gonna go."

"W—"

Her eyes flashed up at mine for a second and then back down. "I gotta get out of this …" She turned and started to walk away.

I took the couple of steps to catch up to her. "Okay, switch shirts and come back."

With her arms fiercely hugging her torso, she shook her head in fast mini-movements. "No."

"Yeah," I coaxed. "The real fun is only beginning. Sam and Olivia are on their way, more people are coming, and we'll have the bonfire out back."

"It's not really my thing." She glanced at the guys. "No." That time it was definitely with more determination. "Thanks for letting me help, though."

"Uh … yeah. Thanks for helping. Are you sure? You sure you don't want to come back? We'll just be drinking, singing, chatting … plain cheese pizza …"

I know she didn't hesitate with her verbal answer, but I felt like I saw a glimmer of one in her sea-like eyes. "I'm sure."

"Well, if you change your mind, just stop up and come out back. Won't even charge ya."

"Why? Because I already gave everyone a peep show?" Her voice was so straight, I had no idea how to react.

"I'm sorry. If I was the one who squirted you, I—"

"It's okay. I'm the stupid one for wearing a white T." It wasn't a smile, but at least I knew she wasn't mad. "Good night. I'm glad you were able to help Sam."

"G'night," I echoed and watched as she—with her arms still so protectively wrapped around her—carefully balanced walking down the grassy hill toward the split-level house that was her dorm.

An odd feeling came over me as I watched Lara disappear. I couldn't exactly pinpoint what it was, but I definitely knew I wanted to find out more about her. She intrigued me—that mix of sassiness, innocence, and realistic outlook on life. And even though she did not come back, I couldn't stop thinking of her that entire night.

CHAPTER FIVE

Finn

On Tuesdays, Sam and Lara had class together. My economics course, which took place at the same time, was a few rooms down, so the three of us began meeting afterward. That, admittedly, was my doing. After the car wash, I had manipulated the meet-ups because of my desire to find out more about the girl from Pennsylvania.

That lead to Sam, Olivia, Lara, me, and sometimes others attending collegiate events, like football games and plays, together. It was during those times I began to realize that what I first thought was stuck-up behavior from Lara was more of a mask or shield to protect herself. From what, though ... I didn't know. Her defenses were evident in her dry humor and the fact she hardly ever smiled. You had to look for it ... know it. There was something so sad and pure about her. She was like a country song come to life.

One Tuesday, while Sam was steps away on a private phone conversation with Olivia, Lara and I were left alone. It gave me the perfect opportunity to ask her a question that had been swirling around in my mind. "I heard about this hush-hush preview right before the real premiere of that new sci-fi film. You know, the third one in the *Star Alignment* series. A couple of the actors will be there signing autographs."

"Really?" Her cheeks rose and her eyes brightened as I'd hoped they might. Lara seemed to like the techy and escapism stuff. Plus, there was a touch of romance in the movie, which all girls fell for.

"Yep. Something about it having been filmed nearby. You wanna go?"

"Yeah." She beamed again. "Let me ask Liv and Sam."

My head surely must have jerked back in shock because inviting others along wasn't the point. It wasn't the plan. I wanted to actually do it … try an actual date with her. It was already taking much longer than with most girls, but that was okay because Lara seemed different.

"They don't have to come," I interceded. "I doubt Olivia will want any part of it. Let's just go … the two of us."

"No, we have to ask them," she insisted.

With incredibly poor timing, Sam was once again at our side. "Ask who what?"

After repeating the movie details to our mutual friend, Lara concluded with, "You and Olivia want to go, right?"

I shook my head behind Lara, willing Sam to understand that I wanted a definite no from camp Olivam. The combination of their names wasn't something I did out loud in front of Sam and Olivia. I did very much enjoy it in my own brain, though. But just as he was oblivious to my nickname, Sam was equally so with my attempt to squash the idea of a foursome. Of … freaking … course.

"God, yeah," Sam exclaimed. "Let's go. I bet we can get a whole crew."

Lara smiled and turned to me. "It's gonna be so cool."

"Uh-huh."

"What? You don't want to?" She noted my solemn disposition instantly. "It was your idea."

"No. I do."

"You don't seem like it," she objected.

"Sorry. Yeah, I do." I ran my hand through my hair, which I had grown out a bit since the whole cancer-patient comment.

"Good. It wouldn't be the same without you." There was her subtle smile again—the rare kind she gave. Her smile and words made me feel a little more wanted and a little less rejected.

"I'm heading up the hill." I spoke of the area where our dorms were. "Want a lift?"

"Sure," she agreed. At least she no longer hesitated when I offered her a ride.

We said good-bye to Sam, who had another class, and made our way to my red Jeep. I was glad to have the extra time alone with her. I wanted to try to broach the date subject again.

As we neared her dorm, I slowed down and suggested, "You know, it would have been fine if Sam and Olivia didn't want to go. *We* could have still went."

"Yeah, yeah, I guess," she said. "But it all worked out."

"We could, though, sometime." I felt like I was stumbling around like an idiot. "The two of us."

"Yeah, I guess." She shrugged and went for her passenger door handle. "Thanks for the ride, Finn."

"Uh-huh. Right."

***

We did go to the movie gig. And despite going with a bunch of people, it was a nice time. Lara liked the special effects of the film. I liked the soundtrack and conversing with the actors.

The good times ended, however, when Sam and Olivia started arguing about something—something stupid and petty. They always did and then would make up almost as instantly. It took away from the evening, though, as Lara and I had to console the couple and take sides.

Since I drove the four of us, I dropped a pouting Olivia off at her apartment and then made my way to Lara's dorm. As she exited the back of the Jeep, I started to get out the front. "I'll make sure you get in okay," I offered. Even though she didn't look at our outing as a date, I liked thinking of it that way.

"The front door is like ten feet away." She plopped her hand on my car door to keep it steady.

"It's ten feet away, dude," Sam—the worst wingman ever—chimed in next to me. Because of their argument, he was going to actually be my roommate and stay at the frat house instead of Olivia's apartment.

"I'm fine," Lara claimed and hopefully did not hear me sigh. "Thanks for setting this up. It was fun. Well …" She leaned in a little closer and, for a split second, I foolishly thought she was going to kiss me. But, of course, she only wanted to whisper so Sam wouldn't hear. "Well, except for Mr. and Mrs. Drama." With that, she shook her head, turned, and walked toward the split-level house.

Lara

I waved a good-bye and "thank you" to Finn as I unlocked and opened the front door to my dorm. It was only after I was inside that he beeped the Jeep's horn and drove away. It was as if he was a protective big brother … it was kind of sweet.

I shrugged off my jacket and climbed the stairs. A few of my fellow dorm mates were in the upstairs lounge— each of them in front of laptops or tablets with earbuds securely in place. Usually that would have been me on a Thursday night. I knew I was going to have to make up some of my work over the weekend, but so be it. It was worth it.

When I opened the door to my room, I found my

roommate, Haylie, lying on her bed in her pajamas with a book in front of her. She took the pencil she was biting out of her mouth and yelled, "Ugh! I hate chemistry!"

"Too late to change majors," was my response to the senior.

"How was the movie thing?" She sat up and asked more calmly.

It was a simple question, but it made me think about how much I had truly enjoyed myself. It was actually hard to remember a time when I had felt so relaxed. I had loved the movie's mix of CG alongside the acting, and the storyline wasn't too terribly cheesy romantic. It actually made me want to know what happened to the couple. Finn had tried to get the possibility of yet another sequel out of the actors, but they kept mum. I think he liked the movie, too. His foot kept rapidly tapping the entire time we were in the theater. With him on one side and Olivia talking the whole time on my other, it had been hard to actually concentrate.

"I had a great time," I finally answered my roommate. "I'm not sure everyone else did, but—"

It was a text from Finn that stopped me. *Tonight was a lot of fun. I'm glad we went. We'll have to do it again minus the …* And he tacked on a pic of the famous dual drama masks.

LOL, I typed back—it was nice to have good friends, and I was glad that over those past couple of months I could count Finn as one of them.

WINTER SEMESTER

CHAPTER SIX

Lara

It was the beginning of the new semester when I got the call. I was in my dorm room, studying alongside Haylie. I didn't even have to look at my phone's screen. I recognized the ring as the one I had assigned my parents. They called about once a week, but it was always in the evenings or on the weekends since that worked better with schedules. So the mid-morning Friday call immediately prompted curiosity if not concern.

"Something's wrong, isn't it?" Haylie questioned. "I can tell. I felt it right before your phone rang. Weird. Want me to stay?"

"No. You and your supposed ESP. Nothing's wrong." The phone rang another time. "Go to class. Good luck on your chem test. Don't blow anything up." *My* first class didn't begin for another hour.

Shutting the door, Haylie left and, with her, so did my childhood. My mother was stoic as she explained across the line that my father had been in an accident the evening before. He and Uncle Jimmy—my dad's brother—were riding ATVs and my father flipped his. Not wearing a helmet, he had severe head trauma and was life-flighted to the hospital. It was the hospital where my mother worked, and she happened to be one of the nurses on duty when they wheeled him in. After dealing with the shock, she was firsthand witness to all of it, including when he passed away in the middle of the night.

"Huh. Uh. Oh," I managed while tipping back a little in my desk chair. "It happened last night, and you're only calling—"

"Lara, so much was going on so fast."

"I didn't even know Uncle Jimmy was in town. What were they doing out on ATVs at night?" The question was a stupid one. Of course I knew. "They were drinking, weren't they?"

"It doesn't matter, does it?"

"No, not when you already know the answer." I should have limited the spite in my voice, but I just couldn't help it. In certain situations, it was a natural reaction of mine.

She ignored it, anyway. "Your brother is on his way. He'll pick you up. Should be there in, I don't know, a couple hours?"

"What? I have to go home?"

"Lara, yeah," she answered directly with a definite note of shock. "You have to come home."

"I have school."

"It's your father." That time her tone was even stronger.

I wasn't thinking straight. I knew I needed to go home. My world was swirling. I had been isolated from all of the chaos of rural Pennsylvania for so long that I didn't want the ugly moth to emerge. But I knew I needed to be there for my mother because, God bless her, despite all of my father's faults, she had loved the man.

"Wait … where's Lane?" My older-by-a-year brother had lived on the East Coast since he graduated from high school. "When did he find out?"

"I called him last night. He's driving in." She had called Lane immediately. She waited to call "vulnerable" Lara.

I pushed that aside, trying instead to think of what my mother was going through. "Okay. I'll get my things ready here."

After hanging up, I moved in slow motion, gathering my bright pink duffel bag and stuffing in items for my passage back home. Not wanting to interrupt her test, I left Haylie a note to let her know I would be gone for the extended weekend. She always went home every weekend, anyway, so it wasn't like it really mattered.

My brother called and said he was about an hour out from picking me up. We didn't speak much. But what was there to say? We both felt the same. We both … felt … the … same.

I decided to call Olivia's landline to leave her a message since I knew she was in class, also. We usually met up sometime over the weekend, so I wanted to let her know that wasn't going to happen. Instead of getting Liv's voice mail, though, Sam answered. He offered his sympathies and said he and Olivia would try to be at my dorm to see me before Lane arrived.

Feeling as if I was suffocating in my room, I decided to go to the lobby area and buy a pop from the vending machine while I waited. The house was in its quiet mode since so many were in class. *I* was in my foggy mode, thinking of, well … absolutely nothing. I should have been thinking of my father or my mother, but I simply wasn't thinking. I was lost in an abyss of cranial haze.

Finn

After a few other unsuccessful attempts at trying to get Lara to go out with just me, I had gotten the it-wasn't-going-to-happen point. What I didn't understand was why.

Because the irony was, when we did go out with friends, she and I pretty much hung out exclusively and joked and talked, anyway. But I learned to accept that we had entered the friend zone. It wasn't necessarily what I wanted, but Lara obviously liked it that way … and I guess it could have been worse. That friendship, more than anything else, was exactly what Lara needed when she literally bumped right into me.

"Finn."

"Hey," I replied softly.

"My dad died." She was blunt and controlled but quiet. I had never seen Lara get really emotional. She was always stoic. And right then didn't seem any different.

If *I* had been told the devastating news she had just relayed to me, I would have been absolutely destroyed. I would have been crying like a baby. I brought my head down the tiniest of bits to look her more directly in the eyes. "Yeah, I know. I was with Sam when you called for Olivia."

"Oh." She backed up a mini-step and started playing with some coins in her hand.

"I thought I'd come see you since Olivia is in class."

"Yeah," was her solitary reply.

"Lar, what happened … with your dad?"

"It was an ATV accident." She had the slightest look of disgust on her face and her voice turned harsher. "I don't want to talk about it."

It was then I realized, besides the basics, she never talked about her family. "You sure?"

"Finn …" Her voice dropped off and was much softer.

It made me want to hold her … *need* to hold her. I wanted to take all of her pain away. So I did. I wrapped my arms around her. Miraculously, she let me. She was usually so reserved and didn't want any kind of help. So it took me by surprise … but in a good way. It felt as if we were in a cocoon, where only I could shelter her from the pain of the outside world—as if I was the one friend she needed.

"You're going home, then?" I asked from above her head and behind her back.

"Yeah. My brother is on his way." She broke our embrace. "I was going to get something to drink from the machine."

It startled me a little. She was back to being brave, strong, and more remote. But since I had gotten to know Lara better, I realized it was just her way. She was good at putting up walls.

"You okay?" I asked.

"Yeah," she answered in a simple and distracted way. Then she did something else which was typical Lara—she changed the subject. "I thought you were going home this weekend. Shouldn't you be heading out?"

"I will."

"Louisville is a few hours away. You should probably get going."

"Lara, you and your promptness." I smiled and teased. "It's only my mom's birthday. It doesn't matter if I'm late. She'll be happy I'm even there. I can stay with you until your brother or Olivia gets here."

"Yeah?" Once again, she had that endearing Lara vulnerability about her.

"For sure."

She nodded her appreciation. "I'm kind of cold. I'm gonna go get a warmer top. I'll meet you in the lounge?"

"What about your drink?"

"Huh?"

"The coins?"

"Oh, can you get it for me?" She handed me the money.

"Yeah. What do you want?"

"Doesn't matter." She started to turn but paused and said, "Thanks, Finn."

"Lara …" I wanted to ask her again how she was, but I knew she wouldn't give me much. "You're welcome."

Sam and Olivia arrived shortly after, and her brother

wasn't too far behind them. There wasn't time for any extensive introductions since the siblings needed to be on their way. So, instead, I gave Lara a quick hug, and she reciprocated with her blink-of-a-smile back. And then she was gone.

CHAPTER SEVEN

Lara

When Lane entered the dorm lounge, a veil of gray seemed to wash over the room. It wasn't because it was an extremely overcast, chilly day. And it wasn't seeing him, either. It was what he represented—going home.

Rimmed with dark circles, which could've only been caused by exhaustion, my brother's eyes looked from me to my three friends, and back to me again. As I stood, Finn did, too. Then Olivia and Sam joined us.

When I made the introductions, Lane was polite but, at the same account, seemed worn. "If you're ready, Lara, we still got a bit of a drive."

"Yeah. Yeah, uh, sure." I picked up my duffel.

Olivia gave me a quick hug and Finn followed with a tight, semi-lengthy one also. I didn't want to leave my friends. They felt secure. They felt more like home than "home" actually did.

But I knew I needed to go. It was only right. My brother had driven all that way to be there. If Lane could do it, I could, too. That was the one good thing about what happened—I got to see my brother.

"I'm not used to driving roads like these anymore," he said once we were on our way. "At least the weather is okay."

The one-lane country road curved, bumped, and twisted as he drove. I couldn't help but find it ironic. It was a great analogy for my life.

"You would be if you ever came home."

I made the statement as a fact ... not out of spite. Because, more than anyone, I understood my brother's need to stay away from our parents' home. Lane had been the one thing growing up that had held me together. And him leaving before my senior year in high school, proved how true that was. He didn't know what a disastrous turn my life took, and I didn't want him to. I didn't want anyone to ever know.

"The old, mean, green machine can't make that long of a trip too often." Lane tapped the top of his car's dash a couple times. It was the same car he had since turning sixteen.

I rolled my eyes at his fib and asked, "Do you remember when you first let me drive it?"

"Hmmm," he murmured. "Pure necessity."

"To get out of—"

"The hell hole. Yeah." He looked over at me in a way that only siblings who had been through so much together could—the extra words not needing to be spoken. Lane was the one who taught me how to drive because he wanted me to always have a way to escape. "And you did. I knew you could. You're in a good school with good friends and everything. That guy ... he's your boyfriend?"

"Sam? No!" I *pfffed*. "He's Olivia's boyfriend."

"No, the other."

"Finn?"

"Finn? What kind of name is Finn? That's like the body part for a fish. What's his brother's name ... Gil?"

"Lane! No." I shook my head. "He's just a friend."

"Hmmm." As I wondered what his non-word meant,

my brother spoke again. "You wanna drive? I have been for so long, I could use the break. As soon as we find a spot, I can pull over."

I'm sure my eyes lit up. I didn't get to drive much. Even though I was saving every penny, I couldn't yet afford a vehicle of my own. "As long as I don't have to parallel park," I answered. "I'm totally game."

"I'm pretty sure you at least don't park crooked and on the damn grass because you're too wasted to do otherwise."

While saying something like that would have been a normal give-and-take between us siblings, it felt a little weird to be talking about our father that way, considering the reason Lane was even with me in the first place. But that was the truth of it. That was—had been—our father … our life growing up.

"Or yelling so loud the neighbors could hear." I found myself adding to the conversation.

"Over shit like what time dinner was. And blaming it on Mom. Like she had any say in anything."

"God, Lane, I thought you were going to absolutely throttle him that night right after your injury."

"My f-ing scholarship to get into college was lost like that." He snapped his fingers. "No money, not good grades, and it was already spring. And *he* was up my ass about going out on a school night. Like it mattered."

"Well, I had to listen about it the entire time during dinner that night."

"Sorry about that." I knew he spoke the truth because my brother had always tried to protect me from the demons at home.

"He was worried about you when you didn't come home, though." I recalled being in my bedroom and listening to my dad downstairs yelling about calling the police because Lane wasn't home—that was how he showed his concern.

"Hmmm."

"He also gave you money when you left to help with your move and hold you over while you looked for a job."

When Lane took off after his high school graduation, he had no real game plan. I know he struggled. But he refused to give up or return. He had since landed on his feet with a job in food service for a hotel and an apartment he could afford.

"I mean, he did feel remorse," my brother admitted. "It was often too little, too late, though. The money did help. And so did Mom's care package of—"

"Chocolate chip cookies." I smiled—our mom was notorious for humming and cooking through her feelings, and those cookies were her favorite go-to.

In the minute or two of silence that followed, a strange sense of sadness seemed to invade Lane's car. It kind of shocked me, but it shouldn't have. Lane and I were going home for our mother. We needed to support her. We needed to be her *emotional* care package.

I realized we were going home for our father, though, too. In hindsight, sadly, not everything had been so horrible. Both of us siblings had a similar relationship with our dad. At different times, one of us might have had it worse than the other. Admittedly, though, the man had always been there—good, bad, and ugly. He had even been there in my darkest days.

After we switched seats in the car, we talked about forgiveness but acknowledged it was easier to talk about than actually give. We also talked about closure. Because, most of all, I think that was what we were going home for.

Finn

"It's sure good to have you back." Mikah slapped me on the arm before clinking his shot glass with mine.

"Thank my mom for having a birthday." I swallowed the bourbon quickly and slammed the glass to the bar.

My former high school buddy mimicked my motion and saluted. "Happy birthday, Mrs. Murphy!"

I laughed. "I love this bar. It has such a buzz." I spoke of the Louisville establishment.

"I think maybe *you* are the one with the buzz."

"Ha! Ha! Yep."

"I'm gonna go take a whiz." He clamped his hand down on my shoulder as he stood. "Be back in a flash."

When I swirled my head to look at the dance floor, I could definitely feel the bourbon and beers in which we had been partaking. Buzzed might have even been turning into actual drunk. At least it was a good feeling.

That was in contrast to what I felt every time I looked at my phone—as I did once again right then—and saw there was still no reply to my text to Lara. I had tried her the night before and earlier that day just to see how she was doing. My heart hurt thinking of what she was going through in her own hometown. But … nothing. No reply. Not even an emoji of any sort—thumbs up, thumbs down, sad face, whatever. I knew, of course, there were many possible reasons for the nonresponse, but I let it get to me, and I realized it was just another way we just weren't on the same page.

"Hey there." A redhead looking to be about my age spoke as she approached. "My friends are all wrapped up in their electronics and I want to dance. You looked pretty good out there earlier. Care to join me?"

I hesitated only for the slightest of seconds and then, putting my own phone away, said, "Absolutely." I loved to dance. I loved to sing. I loved everything about music. Plus, I needed the extra distraction the alcohol hadn't yet secured. I lowered myself from the barstool and took her hand. "Finn."

"Audrey," she returned the name introduction.

The song the DJ was playing was definitely fast and even more so, loud. So the instant we stepped onto the dance floor, Audrey and I became a part of the music. She was a good dancer, mixing it up but exactly on beat. I liked bringing her close to my body but also separating to mirror each other, without a word being said over the pure volume of the tunes. And when a slow song came on, she didn't shy away. She gave me a one-nod, and I took her in my arms. Her head rested on my shoulder and my hands on her expertly fitted jeans.

She pulled her full hair to the side. "Never saw you here before. Do you go to school—?"

"Just home for a visit."

"Oh." I was pretty sure that was disappointment in her voice. "Where—"

"College … in West Virginia. You? I guess you go to school here." The bar seemed to be mostly host to University of Louisville patrons like Mikah.

"Yep. Senior."

"Me, too."

"You got the moves, West Virginia."

"Musician," I explained with pride.

I swear her eyes glistened, although it was a little hard to tell with the eye make-up and mascara she had surrounding them. "Communications major." She pointed to herself. "I'm all about the performing arts. Want to get into broadcast."

I nodded before making the offer. "How 'bout I buy you a drink?"

"I can buy my own, but yeah … yeah, I'd like that very much."

As we made our way to the bar, I noticed Mikah sitting with a bunch of guys at a booth. So I didn't feel too bad for abandoning my buddy. In fact, I felt the opposite. It was nice sitting with and getting to know Audrey, whose outgoing, kind personality was refreshing. It seemed we had so much in common … from dancing to career goals. We exchanged numbers and agreed West Virginia wasn't that far of a distance. And then there was one more thing that clicked. Before she said good-bye, her lips found mine

… and, dang, was she ever a fantastic kisser.

After that weekend, Audrey and I decided to keep seeing one another at least every other weekend. I would make the effort to drive to Louisville and spend time with her. And my friendship with Lara was still intact, especially after I found out she had forgotten her phone on campus when packing for her trip home. It was weird how it all played out, but I was holding on to the fact that things usually happened for a reason.

SPRING SEMESTER

CHAPTER EIGHT

Finn

Shortly before graduation, I found out I'd been selected for a coveted internship at a major record label in LA. It was so surreal and so unbelievably life-changing, I could hardly stand it. Not only was my personal life going splendidly, but the career I had dreamed of was getting a great start, too.

My friend Decan and I decided to celebrate our impending graduation and futures not long after I heard the exciting news. The celebration included a bit more alcohol than we probably should have had. But, we were both friendly, happy drunks. Besides, we didn't do it regularly. So it was all good.

When we decided to call it a night, I helped walk Decan back to his dorm because that's what friends are for after all. The front door of the split-level house dramatically swung open as if we were royalty making a grand entrance. We both laughed at the action and launched sloppily up the stairs.

When I heard her voice, it startled me. I hadn't expected anyone to be sitting there in the second-floor living area. Yet, there she was on the blue sofa, looking right at us.

"Hello, boys."

"Lara ... hello," I slowly echoed back while still supporting Decan.

"What are you two doing?" She shook her head and covered her mouth with her hand, as if holding in laughter.

"Decan here is being all poli-sci guy. We were tossing the pigskin around ala Kennedy. He's trying to drum up business."

"You were playing football, now?" She emphasized the last word in obvious reference to the late-night hour.

"Yep," I answered, holding in a giggle.

"Here, Lara." Decan gave Lara, his housemate, a button with his name on it. "Vote Mickelson for Mayor."

"That really is so cool, Decan. I can't believe you're actually doing this."

Decan was running for mayor in his hometown. His campaign would be in full force upon graduation. If he won, he'd be the youngest mayor in his town's history. If he didn't win, his fallback option was the Navy. With his closely cropped, nearly white hair and circular glasses, he fit the part of both and would, without a doubt, succeed in whichever career.

"Uh, Lara, thank you for my vote." He was still holding onto me. "Um, your, uh—"

"No new taxes!" I quietly egged him on as Lara went to shut the doors leading to the bedrooms. Maybe we were louder than I'd thought.

"No, no new taxes," Decan echoed. "Just for the middle class or the lower class or—"

"I'm recording this," I teased.

"This is my first beer, I swear. I wouldn't lie to my constituents." He looked straight at Lara.

"I don't live in your town or state for that matter," she said and reclaimed her seat on the sofa. "Besides, I'm not registered."

The exasperation in my sigh was noticeable and immediate because I dreaded what was, without a doubt, going to come next. "Oh, boy."

"What?" Decan bellowed. "You're not registered to vote?"

I rolled my eyes at Lara as she replied, "No."

"How can you not be registered?" Riled up, Decan took a step away from me and stood on his own. "That is your duty … your duty as an American citizen … your right."

"I just never did. I had a lot going on when it was time to vote and I was eighteen. And now I'm here, away from home—"

"You need to register to vote, Lara. You can get an absentee ballot," Decan bounced right back. "There's no excuse. It's—"

"Hey, Susan B, settle down. Give the girl a break." I patted Decan's shoulder, trying to mediate between my two friends.

"Pretty good, there, Finnster. Susan B Anthony did advocate voter's rights … women's rights. All the more reason—"

"I do listen sometimes in class, numb nuts," I jabbed.

"Don't be a hater, man. I gotta bounce, anyway. Going to call the old lady."

I disliked that term for girlfriend and debated on whether to tell the budding politician that he should be a little more politically correct, but I was cut off by Lara. "Good night, Decan."

While Decan made his way toward his room, I plopped my drunk ass down next to her. "Why did you have to provoke him?"

"It's like one in the morning. I wasn't thinking." She curled her mouth up at one side and mockingly shook her head.

Covered by black sweat shorts, she moved her legs so they mimicked mine outstretched on the coffee table. I couldn't help but think how far we had come since the first time we'd met. She had directed her legs away from me that initial time in Sam's car. And now, it was almost the opposite.

Replaying our first meeting, I offered the red Solo cup in my hand to Lara. "Drink?"

"Neh."

"Neh?" I spurt out, thinking it was a funny word.

"Not thirsty. Besides, I don't really like beer. Why drink it if you don't like it? I could never understand that."

"You don't drink too much do you, Lar?" That certainly hadn't changed.

"I drink." She sounded offended. But, she didn't drink—not like how ninety-some percent of college kids did.

"I'd like to see you drunk. I mean, really drunk." The crazy idea of seeing her let down all of her inhibitions invaded my mind. "I'll have to take you to the bar some time and line up shots."

"It wouldn't affect me. It's all mind over matter." She reminded me of a cartoon character the way she tapped her forehead, but I didn't want to offend her by laughing.

"Not a chance," I said instead. "I'd pay to see you drunk. Not buzzed—drunk."

"Well, it's not going to happen tonight."

"Yeah, probably not. More for me, I guess." I proved it by swallowing another solid swig. "What are you doing out here, anyway?"

"Checking out the scenery, counting the drunk graduates-to-be, thinking how much it sucks that it's not me."

"Offer stands. We can get you drunk." I smiled, still amused by the thought of Lara drunk.

"Not the drinking—the graduating." She laughed and showed me her visibly swollen thumb. "I got bit by something."

"Youch! What the hell did that?"

"I don't know. I guess spider? It actually woke me up. I was sound asleep and felt the pinch. I'm just keeping an eye on it—making sure it doesn't get any worse. I'm not really anxious to get back into my room."

"I don't blame you. That's nasty."

"Thanks a lot."

"Want me to keep you company for a little while?"

"Sure."

Geez, why did my whole body react knowing she wanted me to stay? I thought I was past the whole thing between her and me. When I mumbled something about having to share the blanket, which was haphazardly draped on her legs, I realized what a guy move it sounded like, and I internally kicked myself.

"You didn't play tonight?" she asked while wrapping her blanket around the two of us.

"Nope." I tried to focus on her question and her face instead of her legs and the proximity the blanket created. "We're done until after graduation. We're going to do a gig in Pittsburgh, though—early summer. Got it lined up. On the South Side. Is that anywhere near where you live? Maybe you could come—bring some friends."

"It's about an hour away. We'll see."

"That would be cool."

"You're still going to LA, though, right?" When she leaned her head on my shoulder, I finished my beer.

God help me, I shouldn't be drinking. I shouldn't be snuggled up against her. It was wrong. Darn it, though, if it didn't feel so right.

"Yeah, at the end of summer," I managed. "I still can't believe it. That place is iconic."

"The best. They had to have really liked the samples you submitted, especially with how steep the competition must have been."

"Well, it is unpaid grunt work."

"But, God, there are hundreds of people who would die for the opportunity. It's your talent."

"And luck."

"How about perseverance?" she compromised. Lara was always my cheerleader. She poked my arm with her index finger. "It's going to open doors. I know it will."

"And, if not, I'll still have my good ole college degree that the folks wanted. I'll have something to fall back on and not just, 'Do you want fries with that?'"

"Finn," she seemed to *tsk*, not going along with my self-doubt. "If anyone can do it, you can. You'll be a big star."

"God, I—" I stopped myself momentarily and probably should have counted to ten. But I didn't. I was feeling good—too good with impending graduation, the internship, the beer, and her ... her support and her platinum locks fanning out on me. I went with the moment and gently lifted her head to face me. "Lara," I said, "if I wasn't seeing Audrey, would you go out with me?" I felt suddenly intoxicatingly high and stone-cold sober at the same time. Even though I pretty much knew and feared the answer—the rejection—I needed to ask the question anyway.

"Finn ..." she hesitated.

I filled the empty silence by sliding my lips onto hers. It wasn't long. It wasn't the best. But it was a first and something I had wanted to do for a long time.

"We would be good together," I concluded while looking at ... searching her eyes.

"You're drunk." She was accurate with that statement but not on her next. "You don't know what you're saying." She didn't give me a chance to reply. "And, you *are* seeing Audrey. You two will move to the West Coast, and you'll forget all about me."

"I doubt it," I admitted out loud.

Needing one last touch, I concentrated on carefully bringing my forehead to Lara's. But that time, our lips wouldn't meet. That was it. It had to be.

I patted her leg. "Night-night, sleep tight, don't let the

bed bugs bite." I think I managed a smile before getting up, walking down the stairs, and exiting back into the coolness of the dark night.

Lara

My mouth must have hung open for a good few minutes after he left. That kiss … his words … they were so out of the blue. Where did all of that come from?

I questioned it, but, in reality, I knew. "Drunk," I even spoke it out loud in a way to totally convince myself. "He was drunk." I knew not to trust drunk.

But he was Finn. He wasn't mean or hurtful or out of control. The soft features of his face had portrayed his compassion and kindness, which mimicked his voice when he spoke. And when I denied what he was saying, he hadn't pushed. He wasn't that guy.

As I sat for many more hours on the sofa, simply staring at the painting of a solo tree, more questions came. Even though it was out of the blue and the alcohol probably made him say things he didn't mean, did I like what happened? Did I want him to pursue or try again? Could there be more than friendship? My thumb no longer hurt but my brain did.

CHAPTER NINE

Finn

"Ugh—the light. Why is it so bright?" I squinted and threw my forearm across my eyes.

I felt as if I was in a vacuum. There was a low buzzing sound in my ears. No, it was more like my head.

When I finally adjusted to my surroundings, I realized I was in my bed. The sheets were tousled and thrown. The pillows laid haphazardly on the floor. I could hear some of my fraternity brothers talking in the nearby lounge. I could tell it was probably closer to mid-day than morning by the slightest ray of light, which beamed a little too brightly through the crack in the window's drapes. My stomach swished a little. And then I remembered. I remembered the night before.

"Oh, geez. Oh God. Lara," I mumbled to myself.

What had I been thinking? Why had I kissed her? I knew "us" wasn't going to happen. I hadn't even felt that way for a while ... since Audrey and I had become serious. Was there some validity to alcohol being a truth serum? What was it about Lara that messed with my mind ... or was it my heart?

It didn't matter, though. In the light of day—the obnoxious bright light of day—it didn't matter at all. Everything was back to how it had been. Well, besides my head. That still needed the help of pain meds or, at least, water.

As I slowly recovered from my hangover by lounging around the frat house, it bothered me more and more what had happened the night before. It wasn't so much about the kiss itself. No. It was the fear that I could have offended her or changed our friendship in any way.

Sometime after dinner, I sucked it up, ran my hands through my hair, put on my "big-boy pants," and ventured down to her dorm. The place was practically empty, as underclassman had started going home for the summer and the others were, no doubt, at one of the local establishments. Lara wouldn't be at either, though. I knew that. I knew her.

Sure enough, I found her in her room. Her door was half-way open, and she was lying on her bed with her back to me. There were only two elements of light—her active, tiny television set and her red lava lamp bubbling away in her window.

I smiled and softly chuckled at the latter of the two. It gave me my opening. "Lar-a, you don't have to put on the red light. Lar-a," I sang the famous Police song, changing Roxanne to her name.

It had been an ongoing joke between the two of us. The lava lamp had instantly sparked the song in my head when I had first seen it in her room months before. Lyrics often invaded my mind like that. It drove my family crazy. The irony of those particular Police lyrics in connection to my blonde friend was downright hysterical. Associating Lara Faulkner with the red-light district was completely out of the realm of sane possibilities.

"Lara?" I tried again, this time without singing, but she didn't move. "Lara?"

I didn't venture any further than the initial doorway of

her room. Again, it was a respect thing … a raised-up-right thing. She didn't turn around. In fact, she didn't move. Of course I knew she was breathing. The slight rise and fall of her back had changed when I had first sung out her name. Was she sleeping? I wasn't sure. She could have been. But, something … Was she purposefully ignoring me … feigning sleep?

God, I knew it. I had really messed up. Only days until graduation, and I had screwed up my friendship with Lara. She not only didn't want to kiss me, but she didn't even want to talk to me or even acknowledge my presence.

Feeling the sting of now being rejected two different times, I retreated from her doorway and proceeded straight to Fat Boys—the nearest campus bar. I thought about pounding a few beers, but I had learned my lesson from the night before. Instead, I took refuge in my true healer. I put my name on the list for karaoke.

"This," I announced to the bar patrons when it was my turn on the stage, "is for all those girls who are just out of reach." I proceeded then to sing "Rhiannon."

After taking my bow, I gave in and drank one beer with a couple of my friends, ignoring their questions about my song choice. I then promptly exited and headed back to the area that housed both my fraternity and Lara's dorm. The red light was off in her window—extinguished.

Lara

I chickened out. There was no other way to describe what happened when I heard Finn's voice nearing my doorway. I wasn't expecting him, and, therefore, I wasn't prepared to face him and what had happened the night before … the kiss. But the truth was, had he told me he was coming, I still probably would have found a way to avoid it … him … the whole thing. Avoidance, pushing things away, and attempting to forget were all things I had become an expert in. So doing it one more time shouldn't have fazed me.

I kept up the guise of sleep long after I knew he had left. And eventually, I got up, closed the door, and turned off the lava lamp. The show I had been watching on TV had long since ended, but I had no idea what had happened from the moment I had heard his "La-ra." My sole focus had been Finn.

So I tried to concentrate on other things, like looking up the ten-day weather forecast and texting my mom since I had missed her call earlier. *Are you at your late shift?*

Just got here. She instantly confirmed what her voice mail had said about her work schedule. That text was quickly followed by another. *I can talk 4 a few. I'll call.*

Before I could refute her offer, my phone rang. I wasn't expecting to actually talk with my mom, but subconsciously I knew it was why I had reached out in the first place. My mom was a worrier, but she was also a great listener ... and secret keeper.

"Hey, Mom," I answered while wrapping my blanket around me. "You didn't need to call from work. Sorry."

"No ... no. I love hearing your voice. I don't get to talk with you enough. How was your week?"

"Good. Good, I guess." I peered out my window where I could see Finn's frat house bedroom—his room appeared completely dark, and I wondered where he had gone.

"You're all done with everything?" my mom asked.

"Yeah, just sticking around to see my friends graduate."

"Anything else exciting happening?"

Well, one of my best friends just blew up my world by kissing me, and I am so confused. "I don't know. Maybe. I guess." I tugged the blanket harder—it was the same one I had shared with Finn the night before.

"Is it about—Oh, gosh, Lara, honey, I am so sorry. They are paging me. I gotta go. We'll talk soon, okay? I'll *see* you soon. It's so lonely here."

"All right, Mom. I understand." It was lonely *here,* too.

I hung up, and my mind went right back to Finn. I knew he most likely had come to the dorm specifically to see me, since there was hardly anyone else there at that time. And I was pretty sure he wanted to talk about the night before. *He* wasn't a chicken. He was brave. He always was—just getting on a stage and saying one word to a room full of people was impressive, nonetheless singing. Coming to my room meant he wanted to confront what had happened. He had tried, just as I had questioned myself if I wanted him to the night before. Once again, though, I had backed away.

CHAPTER TEN

Lara

Olivia's smile mimicked the sunny West Virginia day. It wasn't just because she and so many of my friends had just received their college diplomas. It was because of the solitary gem adorning her ring finger.

"Wow, that is beautiful," I acknowledged my friend's engagement. "How did he ask? Were you surprised?"

I pretty much knew the answer to my second question. We all knew marriage was definitely in the cards for Olivia and Sam. It was just a matter of when. And even though their relationship was definitely a rocky one, they were committed to and counted on one another. The romantic side of me loved the thought of that. The realist in me, though, doubted its very existence.

"I totally was!" she exclaimed. "He did it at the restaurant last night in front of both of our families! I don't remember what *he* said, I just know I said yes."

"Of course you did." I smiled back at my friend.

"It's tiny, I know." She looked at the stone. "But we have to save money, and then Sam promises we'll get an upgrade. Maybe our five-year anniversary. Come on," she changed the subject, "let's take a selfie, okay?" She wrapped her black graduation-gowned arm around me and stuck out her phone for a photo.

"Ugh." I grumbled, hating photos. At least I got to tuck my hair behind my ears and smooth my black and white polka-dot dress before she took the shot.

"Bride and bridesmaid," she pronounced.

I looked at her. "What?"

"Yeah, right? Right, Lara? You'll be my bridesmaid, right? Sam already asked Finn. We can't do it without you."

"Yes you could." I shook my head. "But, yes. Yes, I'll be your bridesmaid."

"Great. You're the best. We're planning on August."

"Oh, right away."

I don't know why I was surprised. Everything moving fast all the time did seem very Olivia and Sam. Or, as Finn called them, Olivam. He swore me to secrecy on that, though. I internally chuckled just thinking of him and that appropriate name.

"Yeah, but the wedding will be before you have to be back here."

She wrinkled her nose as if suddenly campus had a smell. It didn't to me, though. If I put a scent to college, it would be something wondrous like coffee sweetened with honey. I wondered if that analogy would continue, though, with so many of my friends leaving.

That was when I spotted Sam's groomsman, standing a good few yards away. I felt a surge of heat streak across my face. A flashback of his kiss pierced my brain, as if I didn't know what the sudden temperature increase had been about. I hadn't seen Finn since then. Olivia told me he had made a sudden, quick trip to Louisville in between the days of me seeing him at my dorm and graduation. And I saw right then what he brought back from his trip home. The redhead adhered to his side was surely Audrey.

"I gotta go. Sam is over there with his family. He's

waving for me," Olivia announced. "I think *my* family already split." She threw me into another quick embrace. "I'll talk with you later. We have dresses and flowers and, well, all kind of things to discuss."

"Okay."

I had to go, too. I couldn't put it off. I couldn't pretend to be asleep watching television again. I needed to at least say hi—and bye—to Finn.

Finn

Once the graduation ceremony had officially finished, I was officially a man. What a weird feeling. It was both exhilarating and as scary as hell.

"We want to take a family photo near the campus gates." My father's voice was uncharacteristically terse and I wondered why.

Regardless, I obliged. "Okay, Pop. We'll meet you there in a couple."

"Family," he reiterated and then softened. "Maybe you can take it?"

"Yeah, sure," my girlfriend agreed to his request.

As my parents left, I suddenly found myself in front of Lara. My stomach did a quick flopping motion … sort of like those first few seconds or so when I would step on any stage. Her turquoise eyes met mine, and I felt it. It wasn't my imagination. We were both thinking of our kiss on the sofa. Geez, and now I was standing in front of her unable to say anything … unable to apologize or offer an explanation. I couldn't—not with Audrey right there next to me.

Lara broke the strange awkwardness by removing an envelope from her purse. When she handed it to me, I released Audrey's hand. Unleashing the seal, I pulled out a simple graduation card with a McDonald's gift card inside.

"For your long drive to La La Land," she explained. "I

figured there's always a Mickey D's somewhere to stop at along the way. You can get coffee, or a sundae, or those Grimace cookies—but no fries with that." I smiled as she joked about the comment I'd made that night on the sofa.

"Thanks." I tucked the cards back inside the envelope. "And no. No fries." When a bit of awkward silence followed, I asked, "Do they still make those cookies?"

"Oh, I don't know." She looked to Audrey, as if she could provide the correct answer.

The visual of the two girls standing in front of one another made me realize they had never met. Audrey had been on our campus only once, and we had kept pretty much to ourselves that weekend. I liked it that way. Lara, I was sure, knew who Audrey was because of me talking about her and some pics I had. But Audrey? No. It didn't go both ways.

"I don't know. I don't really eat at McDonald's." Audrey's reply drew me back to the topic at hand.

Well, that was true. Audrey was not the fast-food type. She always dressed and groomed herself to perfection. She presented herself in the role she wanted as a career—a television news anchor or something similar. So sticky booths and bouncy kids were not the ideal eating locale for her. Plus, I knew she watched her weight. Whenever we went out, she was a typical salad date—and not *my* salad bar variety. The camera puts on extra pounds, after all.

"I'm Audrey, by the way." She stuck out her hand to shake Lara's.

It was only a split second, but it felt like forever waiting to hear what Lara's response would be. "I know," she said plainly and offered her own name. "Lara."

"Lara," Audrey restated. "Finn, did—"

I didn't wait for whatever question Audrey was going to ask. Instead, I jumped right in with a statement of my own. "So, I'll see you before LA, though," I told Lara as I felt Audrey stroke and reclaim my hand.

"Huh?" Lara's nose scrunched up in confusion.

"You know about the big wedding, right?" I rolled my eyes. I couldn't help it. Even though my bet was on the marriage not lasting, I'd agreed to be Sam's groomsman, and I knew they wanted Lara to be a bridesmaid.

"Just heard. I can't even imagine how that is going to go." Her sarcasm was apparent and mirrored my thoughts to a T.

"And don't forget the gig in Pittsburgh," I reminded Lara.

"Oh, right. Yeah. Send me the details. I'll see."

She didn't seem so sure, though. Her response was very hesitant. Sadly, I wondered if our friendship was witnessing one of its last moments.

As if almost to confirm, Lara said, "I should go. I haven't seen Haylie since she got her diploma, and I want to before she leaves."

I grasped onto Audrey's hand tighter. She was my future. She was the person I was moving to California with. She was the girl I loved.

"It was nice meeting you, Lara," Audrey offered.

"You, too." Lara gave me the most innocent and sweet smile before saying, "Bye, Finn."

Opting for a less definitive farewell, I replied with, "See ya, Lara" as she turned and walked away.

SUMMER

CHAPTER ELEVEN

Lara

Summer break was definitely different from those of my previous collegiate years. I actually went home. Not only for a week or so on each end but for the entire summer. That brought a mixed bag of feelings for sure. But it did make the most sense.

I had an awesome summer internship at a software company, whose focus was developing educational products for elementary students. It paid well—better than the camp—and it was great experience for my resume. And because it was within commuting distance, I could live at home and finally have enough money to lease a cheaper, used car.

Having basically lived independently for a few years, it was an adjustment being home with my mom. I know she appreciated having me there, though. I could see how truly lonely she was without my dad. While the house was brick and mortar, it seemed to have a different overall feeling without him there, too. Again … good, bad, and ugly.

Besides going to the internship, I didn't leave the house much. I had no desire to check out the old digs of town or local friends from the past. I hadn't kept in touch with any of them since leaving for college. I was creating my new world—one which I really liked and preferred—and I didn't want the past to intersect or crash into it.

A few weeks or so into summer break, I made a weekend trip to see Olivia. Well … Olivia and Sam. Because, of course, they were living together. They had moved into an apartment near the Virginia school where Olivia was starting her master's program. Sam was job hunting, but an undergraduate degree in English didn't offer a lot of possibilities.

Over the weekend, Olivia's cousin—Jalisa—and I got our dresses for the wedding. We were the only two bridesmaids. I liked Olivia's choice of a two-piece outfit. The top was spaghetti strap and the bottom was a straight, floor-length skirt. Having similar body types, it suited both Jalisa and me beautifully. The red color didn't seem to go with a mid-August wedding, but I still liked the hue. And, best of all, the price was reasonable.

It was what the three of us did later that evening that I did not care for … not one little bit. Jalisa—who was a couple years older and lived in the area—took us to a favorite bar of hers. She knew the bartenders and had reserved a table.

When we got there, a band was playing. It made me think of Finn. I hadn't heard from him since graduation, and that just confirmed my assessment of the night on the sofa—it was simply a drunken mistake on his part. Therefore, it was my goal to let the physical distance between us pack away any emotional tugs my heart had been struggling with.

Olivia didn't bug me to dance. She had learned her lesson. Instead, I "guarded" their purses and drinks at the dark, very set-to-the-side table. Sitting and watching was fine with me, especially because my being there made Olivia happy, and it was equally nice to be with my friend again.

When a guy started approaching our table soon after Olivia and Jalisa returned, Olivia giggled. "Oh, look at the handsome creature coming our way. Too bad I already have this ring on my finger. You don't, though." She nudged me.

"Way out of my league," I answered. "He is gorgeous."

"Right?" Olivia agreed. "That build."

"Those eyes." I acknowledged his clearest of blue eyes.

His hair was groomed to perfection, too. And, as if he had heard my internal thoughts, he ran his hand through his dark-with-highlights locks. When he stood directly at our table's edge, I guesstimated he was over six feet tall.

"Which one of you is Olivia?" the stranger asked.

When Olivia replied, Jalisa gathered her brown wavy hair to one side, leaned over, and whispered to me, "He's supposed to be one of the best strippers around. Don't worry, I'm paying for it, but he's here for all three of us."

Oh. Dear. God. Really?

Then it began. Right there in the corner of the bar. We weren't the only ones to get the strip show—straight down to the thong. There were other patrons who were privy to an eyeful and snapped photos, too. Olivia, Jalisa, and I got the special treatment, though.

When he straddled himself on my seated lap after Olivia, I tried to protest. But the bar was loud and he was big and built. I closed my eyes, trying desperately for the "other Lara" not to scream.

"Uh, thank you, but, uh … thank you." I stood and backed up against the security of the nearby wall.

The stripper looked unfazed and moved on to Jalisa, who was a much more willing participant. Olivia took videos the entire time, thrilled to pieces by the obvious surprise her cousin had unleashed on all of us. When it was all over—amongst applause and hooting—Jalisa took the guy to the bar to buy him a drink.

"Come on." Olivia pulled at my arm while grabbing her purse. "We can't really talk in here."

The muffled music was still vibrating through the walls, but we could, indeed, hear better once we were outside. And I could breathe better. So that was a good thing.

"That was fun," Olivia offered with a close of her eyes and a soft, remembrance smile spreading across her face.

"Glad you liked it." *My* eyes shutting were definitely not for the same reason.

"It's Sam." When I reopened my eyes, I understood what Olivia was talking about. She was looking at her phone. "He's on his way to pick us up … almost here. I texted him right before our little friend arrived. I'll tell him everything. I don't feel guilty, and as long as he knows, it's all okay. Geez, though, Lara, you looked absolutely miserable. What's up with that? You're not engaged or even seeing anyone. You should have totally sucked onto that. I mean, like you said, he was gorgeous and built more than I initially knew!"

"Olivia!"

"It's true! Why didn't you get more dry hump and grind?"

"I …" What could I say? I didn't want to say anything. I did not want to talk about anything sex-related.

Olivia is a persistent gal, though. "Seriously, what is your deal? When was the last time you got some? You and Oystein, right?"

"No."

"I was wondering. I know you were close."

"I mean, we kissed a few times …" It was more like *he* kissed me twice, but saying it the way I did, didn't make me seem like *such* a loser. I really didn't want to talk about it. I rocked my feet back and forth and felt like securing myself against a wall again.

"Hey, are you …? Are you a virgin? I know you like guys. But you are so awk—That's it, isn't it? Why didn't you—"

"I'm far from a virgin, Liv." I really, *really* did not want to talk about it. "Please stop bullying me."

"Lara! God, I … I'm not bullying. I'm trying to be a friend … to help if I can. I'm sorry you th—There's Sam."

I looked in the direction Olivia was. Dressed in very casual, loose jeans and a worn, green, plaid button-down, Sam had good timing. I wanted the current conversation to end, and I also didn't want to be upset with my friend. Olivia had a strong personality; it was true. However, she did mean well. I just didn't want her help right then.

"Hey, ladies." Sam joined us.

"Sam, I have to tell you, there was a stripper." Olivia blurted out her confession right away, and I looked with wide-eyes toward Sam to see his reaction.

"Hmmm … does that mean I get the night off?" Sam asked his fiancée in a teasing way.

"Oh, God!" I let out my exasperation. "Come on, please … really … I am staying at your place."

Sam laughed and spoke into the phone he had been holding up to his ear when he had approached. "Yeah, the girls had a stripper at the bar." He paused and listened to the person on the other end. "That was Lara who said the last thing."

"Who is that?" Olivia questioned.

"Finn."

When Sam acknowledged our mutual friend, a tingling zinged through my body. It was as unexpected as Finn's name had been. And once again I felt like I was on a dance floor … in the spotlight with everyone watching me. That time, however, it was as if they could see my feelings. The weird part was, though, I didn't even truly understand what those were myself. The thoughts I was trying to pack away were quite a wrinkled mess.

"All right, yeah." Sam talked again into the phone. "Catch ya later," he concluded before hanging up.

"Jalisa's on her way out," Olivia noted, putting her phone down and wrapping her body around Sam's.

When my phone vibrated, I brought it out of my purse and looked for the text message. *Olivam & their drama. Some things never change.*

While Finn's text made me smile, there was also another truth—one I had to learn to come to grips with more and more that summer as everything and everyone started moving in different directions. *Some things do,* I typed back.

Finn

Those first couple of months post-collegiate world? Boy, no one prepares you for that. If leaving home for the first time when *entering* college was scary, *after* college was ten times worse. The world was no longer mapped out for you. You weren't constantly surrounded with friends and fun. It was downright frightening and a little depressing.

The good thing was, I had anchors in my life. One, of course, was my family. They always kept me grounded. Another was the upcoming internship, which gave me a direction in which to start my new life. And a third, I had come to realize for sure, was Audrey.

"You're unusually quiet." I noted my girlfriend's disposition from across the room as she strung her legs once again through her panties.

We had spent the afternoon in my room while we had the privacy. But, my parents were expected back soon from their lunch outing with friends. And even though I was an adult, I was still kind of treated like a kid, especially since I was living at home for the summer. That meant they didn't want to see a naked girl in my bedroom … and it wasn't like I wanted them to, either.

"Hmmm." Audrey started buttoning her top. "I guess I was just thinking."

"About?" I prompted, with my sweats now hugging my hips.

"Finn?"

"Yeah?"

"I'm kind of anxious about going to California."

It was the first time I'd heard her actually say that, but I definitely knew where the thought had manifested from. We had visited her parents a week or so before, and they weren't happy about her moving so far away without any stability whatsoever. Audrey didn't have a job lined up as I did my internship, but she was hoping to find something once we got to LA. It was the media mecca after all. She had blown off her parents' reaction when I had questioned her about it afterward in the car. But I had seen the legitimate worry creep into her eyes, and it was truly an oddity for such a strong, tackle-anything girl. I didn't like her feeling that way. I didn't want her to feel concerned at all … not about moving and not about me, which I feared tied into it. So, a couple days after visiting her parents, unbeknownst to anyone, I had found a way to make things all right. I was alone in town and thinking of her, her family's concerns, and that I knew I couldn't live without her. Plus, it seemed like the next step. That was what you were supposed to do—high school, college, job …

I hadn't planned the next part out and certainly not having it take place in my childhood bedroom with both of us half-naked. I had thought maybe once we were in LA and on our own. But, regardless, I walked over to the nightstand and pulled out the box.

"Would this help?" I opened the lid to show her the simple diamond on a gold band, one that I could afford with payments.

Her mouth gaped open and her stare was then completely on me. It had been a complete surprise. Besides casually talking about what we wanted in the future, we hadn't specifically discussed an engagement.

"Are you … really?" she questioned.

When I replied with a full, closed-mouth smile and nodded, she fell into my arms and kissed me. Any uncertainty or nervousness I might have felt about presenting the ring completely evaporated. Seeing her happy made *me* more than happy. I knew I loved her and wanted her with me, but knowing we had a commitment not only gave *her* a sense of contentment and security but I realized it gave me it, too. And that was something I hadn't felt since graduating.

CHAPTER TWELVE

Lara

"Whatcha looking at?" Brenna was peering at my desktop computer.

I hated the open concept of the office where I was working for my internship. It was supposed to promote teamwork, but it was loud and my back was exposed, so people always walked up behind me. Eighty percent of the time I jumped. I was, unfortunately, already known for it.

"I know that bar," my slightly older colleague acknowledged the website on my screen. "A lot of cool, upcoming bands play there. Who is—"

"It's a guy I know from college." I noted Finn's name and the date just days away.

"What's he sing?" She wheeled the nearby green chair next to me and sat.

"Country mostly."

"You going?"

"Eh—"

When Finn had e-mailed about his gig in Pittsburgh, I told him I doubted I would go. I didn't know exactly where the bar was, and I didn't want to go alone. In truth, that was only part of it. Hearing Sam talk with him and getting his text a couple of weeks before had once again brought the singer to the forefront of my thoughts.

Dang it! Why had he said what he did that night in my dorm? Would any of what I was feeling have even surfaced if he hadn't? Because, even the slightest reminder of him carried my confused emotions to the forefront of my mind every single time.

"Eh?" Brenna brought my thoughts back to her.

"I don't know. I'm not sure."

"I'll go. Yeah. If you want, let's go together. I love going into the 'burg. What do you say?"

"I hate driving in the city." I offered the one true excuse I was willing to voice out loud.

"Oh, I can totally drive. No biggie."

"Uh, well, yeah ... okay."

"Fun. Yeah. Cool."

I hadn't planned on it, but the more I thought about it, the more I wanted to. I wanted to see him again. I wanted to be in the same room and try to figure out what my brain was still weirdly screeching about when I gave it a chance. And I'm pretty sure—subconsciously or not—that was what led me to wear a new, sleek, black outfit and more makeup than usual when we went to Pittsburgh that Saturday.

Thank goodness Brenna drove. It made me nervous just being shotgun as she tried street after street looking for a spot to park ... and it was all parallel parking. We would have definitely turned around and gone home if I had been driving.

But she did well, and we eventually made our way into the dark and packed nightclub. The warm-up piano player was finishing a piece—something classical. Brenna immediately went to the bar, and I was so relieved when she ordered a pop. Maybe I could even relax and enjoy myself at a bar for a change. Besides, I already had enough on my mind as it was.

We climbed the steps and stood along the upper balcony rail just before Finn took the stage. It was just him. Finn had officially become a solo act—something he was going to do once moving to California, anyway—since Bryan had taken a "real" job in Canada.

He looked good and, dare I say, might have been gaining groupies the way the first few rows were reaching out to him as he sang. He definitely had stage presence alongside his vocal talent. His looks—especially that smile—didn't hurt either.

Brenna wanted to get closer, so we weaved our way down the steps and tried to inch as close as we could. It was a couple of songs later when Finn spotted me. His smile was quick and slightly surprised, as I hadn't told him I was coming. The grin was most definitely there, though, as he continued to play to the crowd.

Brenna and I stayed until he wrapped and then went to hang out in the lobby so I could introduce her to Finn and, of course, see him myself. It was there that I saw Audrey … and her ring. Oh, God. What? Why hadn't he told me? I felt so incredibly caught off guard.

The rest of the evening was a blur. Finn, sweaty from performing, eventually joined us. He seemed genuinely excited that I came, giving me one of those Finn hugs. But then he immediately kissed Audrey. What made me think it would be different? Why had I even bothered to think at all?

Finn

When one of the swaying cellphone lights tilted toward a person in the audience, it highlighted her face. Standing quite a few feet back was Lara. She had come after all. I did a quick smile in her direction but didn't break my performer mode. It felt like forever since I had last seen her, yet it had only been a couple months—a couple months where so much had already changed.

After the final note was played, I made my way to the small lobby area to meet Audrey. But I also found Lara and another girl who looked to be about our age. "Lar, I'm so glad … shocked," I amended and then continued while giving her a hug, "but glad you're here."

Her response was a tight grasp around my torso followed by an almost-immediate release. She pointed to her shorter, brunette friend. "Brenna made me do it."

A small smile accompanied her obvious effort to joke but neither came off quite right. She seemed a little unsure … more like the Lara I had first met. Well, besides her physical get-up. She wore more makeup than her usual, casual look. It was darker and heavier. And her clothes were more form-fitting than I was used to seeing her in. She looked nice, but didn't really need any of it. Maybe it was her new concert look.

"Congratulations." She swapped her eyes back and forth from Audrey to me as I gave my fiancée a kiss.

"Thanks." I knew I was beaming both from coming off the high of performing to a receptive crowd and having Audrey by my side. "We were going to head straight back to Louisville, but if you want to grab a drink or something …"

"Neh."

I almost laughed again at that little nonsense word. But, I didn't, because it still meant no. I should have guessed Lara would have passed on the drinking, but I still hoped she would have at least wanted to catch up.

"It could be coffee." I offered a "Lara" alternative.

She shook her head. "No. Gotta get home myself. I guess I'll see you in a couple weeks."

"We'll be there." I acknowledged Sam and Olivia's nuptials. "Lara," I said a little slower. "Seriously, thanks for coming. It means a lot."

"Yeah."

She probably thought I was referring to the support all

artists needed. It wasn't just that, though. It was the fact that I realized I hadn't lost her as a friend. She had come. I *hadn't* screwed everything up. I had worried after her blow-off the night after our kiss. And then that was amplified with her brief and cryptic reply to my text when she had been visiting Sam and Olivia. But despite not having a chance to actually talk about it, there didn't seem to be any lasting negative effects from our kiss. Thank goodness because that truly would have meant a country song kind of ending.

CHAPTER THIRTEEN

Finn

Sam and Olivia's wedding took place in Sam's West Virginia hometown. It was an intimate affair. Sam didn't have a big family and Olivia's was a hot mess who either didn't attend or were arguing. There was also the issue of trying to keep the cost down. So, that meant not inviting many friends and having the rehearsal dinner the night before at Sam's parents' home.

I found Lara alone in their downstairs game room when I went to use the restroom. "Hey." I joined her as she looked at the typical tacky family photos displayed on the wall.

"Hi," she replied without even a turn of her head. She seemed so withdrawn and had been for most of the evening.

"Haven't really had a chance to talk with you. Too caught up with apples in pigs mouths," I snarked. "I mean, I know they said simple, but a pig roast rehearsal and no walk-through at the church?" Not that I was complaining about the second part. "What do you think about all of this?" I bumped her on the shoulder in a friendly way and rolled my eyes. "Olivam …" I tacked on.

I expected her to go along with what had been our regular banter about Sam and Olivia, but she didn't. "It's fine."

"Lara …" My voice jolted in shock because she was just turning and walking away. "Where are you going? What—?"

She stopped and swiveled back around. "They're getting married. Let it be." Again, it was said in such a mellow way but also with determination.

"I was—" I was going to say teasing, but she cut me off.

"Finn, everyone makes decisions and commitments, and you have to respect that. That's what I have to do."

"I know. Geez."

She exhaled in a staggered, attempt-at-calming kind of way. "I'll see you outside."

While I used the bathroom, I kept replaying her words. What was with the switch in attitude toward the impending nuptials? And why so serious? It made me wonder if more was going on. But what? Was it even about Sam and Olivia? Lara Faulkner was still so confusing to me.

When I returned to the bonfire, there were only a few of us remaining. After switching the tunes, Sam's brother, Parker, sat next to Lara on one of the built-in benches. I, simultaneously, sat across from them and next to Audrey. When Parker started talking about the song as if he was an authority on the music business, I was instantly annoyed. In contrast, Lara seemed to be taken in by the know-it-all. She certainly was listening quite intently to his opinion on not only the subject of music but virtually everything else. He was a sophomore in college and still an undecided major. What did he know? What did he know about music or life or … anything?

"Why, if you sit any closer to her, you'll need to get some protection." Sam's voice surged into my thoughts, and I realized he was talking to me and how my legs were intertwined with Audrey's.

She, in turn, put her hands on mine where they had been resting right between her breasts and waist. "You *are* quite affectionate," Audrey cooed, echoing Sam's thoughts.

"Just like to be close to you," I responded with honesty, having not even realized my actions. "We're planning a wedding, too." That statement, directed at Sam and the rest of the group, came out a little defensive since I seemed to have critics suddenly surrounding me.

Lara's yawn was long and a bit dramatic. It, and the fact that she started to get up, caught me by surprise. "I'm going to get going," she announced.

"First yawn," I noted. "It doesn't count."

The look she gave me was coated with curiosity, and I couldn't figure out why. Yes, I noticed. I paid attention to things.

I didn't have time to debate or question anymore, though, because Audrey echoed Lara's statement. "I'm getting tired, too."

"I'm screwed." I let out a sigh and placed my half-empty beer bottle down. So much for fun times around the bonfire.

"You hope." Audrey giggled and leaned a little further onto me.

I realized then what I had said and how she had interpreted it. I shook my head and gently tugged on her hand, standing both of us up. "I guess we're outta here." I suggestively lifted my eyebrows twice and tried to push everything else about that night away. The motel and my fiancée were calling.

Lara

I knew I was acting kind of weird or different at the rehearsal dinner party. I couldn't help it. I was resorting back to my most introverted, socially awkward self. The strange part was, I was amongst friends—my nearest and dearest—and I had really been looking forward to seeing them. But when it actually happened, I didn't feel like I belonged.

One of the biggest things was being a solo act amongst the nearly all couple group. Brenna had told me I could have brought her brother as my date. I had never met him, though, so my awkwardness would have been at high peak for sure. Although to have had someone there while the other couples were practically pawing each other might have at least made me feel a little more a part of the group.

"I can drive you to the motel," Parker—the only other single left at the bonfire—suggested after I faked a yawn for an excuse to leave.

"We're already going there." Finn, holding Audrey's hand, instantly offered and took a step closer to Parker and me. "We can take you, Lara."

"Yeah, there's room in my car," Audrey offered.

She really was a nice girl. It was hard finding something wrong with Finn's choice in a fiancée. But, still, I did not want to be in the car with the two of them.

Luckily, there was an easy solution. "I have my own car now, remember?"

"Hmmm. Yeah, right," Finn acknowledged.

"Thanks, though, Parker." I made sure to thank Sam's brother.

"Sure thing. We'll meet up at the wedding tomorrow."

"Absolutely." I smiled back … at least tomorrow was a new day.

Finn's face seemed to scrunch before he said, "Can we at least walk you to your car?"

I wanted to argue that I was capable, but he and Audrey were going that way anyway, and it did seem to be Finn's thing to do … make sure I got in safely. "I guess. Good night, everybody," I said as Finn extended his free arm in a forward direction as if he was protectively showing me the path of escape.

It wasn't that far to the driveway where the cars were parked, but the silence that vibed so strangely between us made it seem that way. It was probably just in my head, though. It was *my* problem after all.

"Good night, Lar." He seemed as though he wanted to give me one of his Finn hugs, but I denied it by opening my car door.

"Good night, Finn. Good night, Audrey."

I entered my car and buckled in. After turning on the engine, I checked my phone and started scanning stations on the radio. It seemed everything was country ... of course. When I pulled out, Audrey did, too, and their headlights were behind me for part of the ride. It was kind of nerve-wracking. At least they stopped at a red when I went through a yellow.

But as luck would have it, I ended up arriving at my motel room around the same time Finn and Audrey did theirs on the same hall. My little detour to the lobby's vending machine probably was the culprit. That meant I had the "great privilege" of seeing the couple enter their room with hands flitting around each other's backs and butts. Oblivious to anything else, they fortunately didn't see me, though.

That was when I realized the other part of my rotten disposition that night. It was one thing to know something. It was a whole other to witness it.

I opened the door to my room, closed it behind me, leaned against it, and took a deep breath. I had told Finn that things change and everyone needed to respect decisions. I decided the way *I* was going to do that was by making a big change of my own.

CHAPTER FOURTEEN

Lara

When Olivia saw me that next day, she practically had a coronary. I didn't care, though, because what I had done felt so liberating … as if I was freeing myself of everything in my life. It was similar to when I had changed schools and dyed my dark strawberry blonde hair platinum. The difference? When I was in my motel room the night of rehearsal dinner, I didn't change hues. I cut it off … more than eight inches of my long hair.

In all actuality, it wasn't a bad job. The cut was pretty even. But Olivia wanted Jalisa's and my hair up in a particular style, and with my new shortened length, it simply could not happen. The hair couldn't be fixed, like so many things in life.

"Why *did* you do that?" Olivia asked after finally calming down at the beauty parlor where she, Jalisa, and I were getting the finishing touches from the glam squad. "What was up last night? You and Finn were both … I don't know … weird."

"Nothing," I answered. "Nothing was up," I automatically denied and then deflected. "C'mon, we don't want to be late getting to the church. You still need to put on that beautiful dress."

I knew the night before had been an emotional mess for me. But, Finn? Something was up with him? *He* had been acting differently, too? I took a deep breath and shook my head, trying to declutter the mental noise that didn't seem to want to go away.

Finn

Poor Sam. He looked dapper in his black tux similar to mine, and his light brown hair had never been more trimmed to perfection. But, he had tears in his eyes as the two of us stood in the groom's room right before the big event. I guess I would have, too, if I was facing a life with Olivia.

I was kind, though, when I offered my support. "What's going on, man?" I asked. "What's going on in that crazy Sam head of yours?"

"Nothing," he said. "Just happy and excited." He went macho then and subtly wiped his eyes before turning the question on me. "What was going on with *you* last night?"

"What are you talking about?"

"I don't know. You were acting strange, and Lara was, too."

"No, I wasn't," I denied. "But, yeah, Lara was for sure, huh?"

"Women …" Sam shook his head mockingly as Parker and their dad entered the room.

It was time to take our places at the altar. Things were ready to become real for my friend. Life, in fact, was definitely starting to be real for all of us.

***

When Lara walked up the aisle after the little flower

girl, my bow tie strained as my neck extended forward and my mouth dropped open. It wasn't the red dress she was wearing. She looked stunning, of course. Geez, though ... her hair. What had she done to those long locks? I had seen her less than twenty-four hours before and ... and ... whoa. What did she do?

Standing across from me, I couldn't help but stare at her. I couldn't say anything, though, of course. We were in the middle of a wedding ceremony and were all supposed to be looking at the next people coming up the aisle—Jalisa and finally the bride herself.

All during the short service, I was formulating what I was going to say to her. I knew I had to be careful. Girls didn't fare well with even the slightest, tiniest comment about their clothes, makeup, hair ... whatever. Audrey was like that, and I knew Lara probably would be, too. But I also knew I had to say something.

After the *I dos*, as the groomsman, I extended my arm out for Lara as we made our way back down the aisle. I waited until we got to the last pew before I whispered, "Rapunzel, what happened? Did the witch find you out?"

She kind of snorted her laugh. That's good, I thought. She was going to take it in the lighthearted way I had intended it to be.

"Someday my prince will come," she replied, and we continued to walk toward the connecting banquet hall where the reception would take place.

"Why, Lar?" I asked as we entered the room. "I mean, it's nice," I tried. "But, wow, it's so short."

Her hair wasn't past her shoulders anymore. In fact, it wasn't even near her shoulders. It barely grazed her chin. She haphazardly tucked a piece behind one ear and said, "I needed a change. You guys are all changing, and since I still have to be in school, I wanted a change, too."

"Hmmm," I mumbled as Parker and Jalisa joined us at the elongated white table meant just for the bridal party.

In a few minutes, the room was filled with guests

including two frat brothers, family, and the newly married couple. The traditional wedding things started to take place instantly. When dinner was served, there were red potatoes and chickpeas with ranch dressing on my plate. I leaned forward a little to note that no one else had that combo at our head table. Sam, who was obviously waiting for my reaction, had a smirk on his face. I did one back.

It was then that I decided to do something impromptu. I snagged a microphone from the DJ, turned it on, and thumped on the mesh, gaining the crowd—I mean, guests'—attention. "I know this is the best man's job, but I want to give a toast, too," I announced while reclaiming my position at the head table.

All eyes were on me. "If you look at my social media—Finn Murphy musician." I smiled at the crowd, getting my little plug in. "I have a lot of friends." I put my fingers up for air-quotes. "But, you will only see the real ones in this room." I nodded to Sam. "Because a real friend knows your favorite foods and secretly adds them to your dinner at his wedding. And … I'm guessing they are going to be even better than the school cafeteria's." I smiled. "A real friend supports you. They listen to your bad ideas, including lyrics, and help you no matter what."

"There were some crappy ones, dude," Sam chimed in loudly.

"Supportive, that's what Sam is," I said with sarcasm and then turned serious again. "He's more than just a frat brother or roommate. Sam's a real friend … even with all his drama." I glanced at Lara and, sure enough, her eyes opened to capacity and her mouth bristled together with a stifled laugh. "It seems like he has found a different roommate, though." I looked to Olivia and tried my best to put on another smile. "I wish them the best." They were going to need it, I secretly thought.

"Thanks, man," Sam acknowledged before Olivia cut in.

"Lara, you should say something, too … before Jalisa."

"Uh, uh, no. I wasn't planning on that." Lara's wiggling intensified as I approached her with the microphone. "Finn …" She said my name almost as a warning.

"Come on," I tried to persuade.

"No. I don't want people to look at me." She was talking softly, but I accidentally hit the mic button back on and her last three words came out across the speakers.

I quickly switched it back off and grinned as I said, "Well, they are now." And I handed her the mic. "Go ahead."

With an eye roll, she flipped the microphone back on and quickly spoke to the guests. "What he said."

The guests laughed. I always told Lara she had a good dry sense of humor. She never got it. Olivia obviously didn't either, as she seemed to scowl at the lack of a speech.

I knew Lara felt awkward, though, so I started to reclaim the mic, but she turned to the guests and said one more thing. "Although, I would have thought as a musician, *his* words would have come out more lyrical. Maybe he should sing." And she promptly thrust the microphone back at me with a smirky smile of her own.

I wrinkled my nose up at her and debated if I should think of something to serenade the group with. But Olivia stood up and took the microphone from me. She was most definitely not one of the supportive friends I counted in the room. The sarcastic blonde with turquoise eyes was, though. Olivia gave the microphone to Jalisa, and then we heard her and Parker's toasts, which were both lame in my opinion.

After dinner, Sam and Olivia had their first dance as husband and wife. Then they announced for the wedding party to join them. I grasped Lara's hand and we strolled onto the dance floor.

She was fine for a moment or two until I drew her closer to me. "This red dress reminds me of your lava lamp, Roxanne."

She suddenly pulled away and signaled for Audrey to join us. When my fiancée did, Lara said, "Here, dance with him. I hate it. You two should."

"You sure?" Audrey asked Lara and then looked inquisitively at me.

"Lar?"

"Enjoy." Her lips twitched up quickly. "I'm on a mission, anyway."

"What? What mission?"

I wanted to understand her sudden motion to extract herself from the dance floor, but, I wouldn't get an answer. The switch had been made. Audrey was snug and comfortable in my arms. She loved to dance—slow or fast, it didn't matter. And I loved dancing with her. But I couldn't help being concerned about Lara's abrupt exit.

CHAPTER FIFTEEN

Lara

When Finn tugged me in closer to him, it wasn't purely a physical draw. It was an emotional one. My body did the tingling thing again, and my mind went a little foggy. Those feelings of attraction were definitely there, but it was too late. It was too late to do anything about it. Finn obviously didn't feel the same way. Audrey standing at the edge of the dance floor was confirmation of that fact for sure.

Oddly, though, her presence helped. Needing to get out of the suddenly stifling situation, I called Finn's fiancée over and requested a swap. She could dance with him. She *should* dance with him. *She* was the one with him.

Besides, I hadn't even wanted to participate in the bridal dance in the first place. But Olivia had done her scoffing laugh when I had raised my objections. So it had been easier to just go along with it.

My clean getaway was thwarted, however, when after grabbing my purse and taking a few steps toward the exit, Olivia stopped me. "Lara, get that photographer. He's not doing his job. I want a photo of us dancing." She squeezed

Sam's side.

Despite being discouraged by the delay in departure, I, nonetheless, did the bride's bidding. But it only aided in making two people disgruntled with me. The photographer did not take kindly to my request, seeing as he *was* doing his job by going around and taking photos of each guest table. Plus, Olivia was upset with me, too, when I wouldn't tell her where I was going. It certainly was not my day—or weekend for that matter.

The fact was, I couldn't tell Liv where I was going. For one thing, it was a surprise for her and Sam. For another, my mission had become twofold. I also needed to regulate my thoughts before everyone became privy to my feelings. I had become a pro at the emotions disguise, and I was determined not to let my record be broken at someone's happy occasion.

When I walked past the bar, the men who were gathered did some kind of collective cheer-grunt and I looked in their direction. There was a boxing match on television. How could it ever be acceptable for anyone to beat someone else up as a sport? No. Just … no.

I walked a little quicker and finally escaped to the brisk nighttime air. It felt lonely and refreshing at the same time. I took a few breaths and made the way to my car. I sat in the driver's seat for a while simply thinking of moments between Finn and me. They were scattered and splintered as if directionless. And that seemed fitting in itself. The good part? They were all positive. But the bad part? It didn't matter. Things were what they were. Everyone was moving on, and that was how it was supposed to be.

Eventually, I got to the real mission and dug the sign out of my car's trunk. Maybe putting my mind on something else, rather than my sorry state, would do some good. I thought it was starting to work when a voice startled me so much I jumped and screamed.

Finn

Her mood, the hair change, and leaving during the dance … it all bothered me. I needed to find Lara. I needed to figure out what was going on. I took a final swallow of my bourbon mix and set out to search for my friend who was apparently still on her self-proclaimed mission.

When I found her, she was outside straightening the strap on her dress and looking at Sam's white car. "Lara, why are you—"

"Ahhh!" she screeched and nearly jumped a mile, turning around to face me. "Finn! You scared me."

"Sorry." I shrugged. "What are you doing out here?" I asked but then saw her handiwork—a "Just Married" sign was draped on the car. "That's cool," I commended. "I didn't know people still did that. Let's hope Olivia appreciates it. She's kind of pissed right now that you're not inside."

"What are *you* doing out here? *You* should be inside."

Her clipped tone made me bend slightly and focus more on her eyes. They weren't filled with tears, but it was something close. There was definitely sadness and pain in them. And it about killed me.

"Lara …"

"You should be with Audrey." She looked down.

"Audrey can take care of herself." I took a mini-step closer. Audrey *could* take care of herself, and I knew Lara normally could, too. But, at that moment, she seemed so lost.

"She's who—"

"Audrey is dancing with Sam's great-uncle," I interjected.

The immediate crinkle between Lara's eyebrows displayed her obvious curiosity regarding the odd dance duo. I smiled the best I could, considering my concern for the girl in front of me. Besides, I truly had nothing to be jealous of with Sam's geriatric family member.

"She caught the bouquet, and he got the garter," I explained.

It was good to see Lara's hand go up to her lips to stop herself from laughing. But, almost as quickly, her reaction changed. She, oh my God, was crying.

"Lar …" I stuck out my hand a little dumbfounded. "Lara, what's … gosh, what's wrong?"

"Go." With her hand then fully up to her face, she turned from me, creating yet another barrier between the two of us.

I didn't want to make things worse or embarrass her, but I was not going to leave. I couldn't. "No," I said softly but confidently and stepped into her line of vision again.

"Finn!" She was more adamant and still refusing to look at me.

"Lara, what? What did I do?"

"You made me—" She halted her words as she dropped her hand but looked to the ground.

"What? I made you give a speech? I think you paid me back." Was that really it?

"No. Not that. You made me …" This time it was more of a pause, and I let the empty air hang until she came up with a concluding word. "Think." She finally looked up to meet my eyes.

"Sorry?" I offered, not exactly sure what I had made her think about. But whatever it was, it must have been bad. "Think about what?"

"Never mind. It doesn't matter. You need to leave."

I shook my head. "No. Not happening."

She took a staggered but seemingly calming breath. "I'm gonna miss all of this." Her voice cracked. She sounded and looked so darn vulnerable—more than I had ever seen her. "I'm gonna miss all of you guys. I didn't realize how much. I guess I should have at your graduation. Maybe it was because, in the back of my mind, I knew this—the wedding—was still coming."

Her words went straight to my heart. They were so true. They were so dead-on. She nailed what I hadn't let myself outwardly acknowledge.

"Well, that's all the more reason for you to be inside with us." I shook my head in a joking way, hoping to lighten the mood.

"You think?" She followed my lead and jested back while pressing her index fingers under her eyes and subtly wiping.

"Uh … yeah." I lightly pushed her bare shoulder, as if we were innocent children playing a game of tag.

"I still don't like dancing, though," she restated and gave me a similar shove back.

I rolled my eyes but let the topic of dancing drop. Just knowing she wasn't as upset or mad anymore and that she was going to rejoin us was enough. It was more than.

"Lara"—I took her hand—"I'm gonna miss you, too. We'll keep in touch." Not wanting to let my sudden tidal wave of sentimentality show, I teased, "Who else is going to help me with my webpage design once I'm all Mr. Rockstar?"

"All your richy peeps." She smiled, and I pulled her to my side before we made our way back into the celebration.

POST COLLEGE

CHAPTER SIXTEEN

Lara

After the wedding, Finn, Olivia, and Sam were all starting new adventures. Not me. I was still going to be at the same place ... doing the same thing. I wanted to get on with my life as they were, but choices had been made in the past—long before college—and I was doing my penance by staying until I could finally graduate. That wouldn't be until December, and it would involve none of the fanfare that my friends had. There would be no crossing the stage, no wearing of the robe ... no friends yelling congrats. The college only conducted a formal graduation ceremony once a year—in May. But December's sure-to-be cold chill seemed somehow more fitting for me, anyway.

I had a number of classes to fit in before, though, which meant my schedule was the busiest it had ever been. I had no time for anything or anyone else. Since I was only going to be there part of the year, the school found me a single room, which helped. Having a roommate would have only been a distraction, especially when it couldn't be Haylie … who was another graduate in the "real world." I felt so misplaced on campus. At least I only had a couple months to get through.

Olivia and Sam came to visit for homecoming weekend in October. It wasn't the same, though. They stayed at a nearby hotel for one night, and they practically made fun of me for worrying about my classes when I was basically already guaranteed graduation.

"Geez, Lara, soak this up. Seriously." Olivia shook her head slightly. "This was the life. Wait until you have bills and more bills to pay and only one job."

"I have a job." Sam knew she was speaking about him. "*You* have the bills."

"A better paying job," Olivia clarified. "And, it was *our* wedding."

"They are *your* cats … and clothes."

There they went—argument number five thousand twelve. Or was it five thousand thirteen? I knew it was minor and they would get over it soon enough, but it made me miss the only real person who would understand the "Olivam drama."

I would have to fill Finn in at some time. Of course it wouldn't be in person or the same as it used to be. But I was glad we still kept in touch with a text or quick phone call here or there. And those seemed better since our talk in the parking lot at Olivia and Sam's wedding. I was terribly embarrassed to have cried in front of him like that, but it was, in a way, needed. I hadn't told him everything … all I was feeling, but I *felt* like I had, and he seemed to unburden a little himself, too. Our friendship was intact. That was, in the long run, what was most important.

Finn

I never truly knew how busy, busy could be until

Audrey and I first moved to our tiny studio apartment in Burbank. She got a job as a page at one of the networks and worked practically non-stop. And I absolutely loved my internship at the record label. I was learning so much, in addition to networking and speaking with people who spoke my music language. Besides the minimal money we made, life was almost too good to be true.

I didn't forget about Lara, though. I just didn't have a lot of time to keep in touch, besides an occasional funny text about drama or technology here or there. But I did call her when I was in a McDonald's using her gift card. While munching on a burger, I informed her the only cookies the restaurant had were circular and not shaped like any characters. She told me I should boycott the chain altogether then. My laugh was hearty as I admitted that I couldn't. I would miss the shakes—particularly the Shamrock ones—too much.

I called her again when I was visiting my family in Louisville during the Christmas holiday. I finally had a chance to breathe and wanted to make sure to acknowledge her December graduation. "Did I miss your graduation, Lar?"

"It wasn't anything," she answered without missing a beat to my opening line.

"Sure it was," I denied.

Typical Lara, she switched the topic from her to me. "It's good to hear from you. Where are you? *How* are you?" The way she said those words, with a light bounce in her voice, made me know, without seeing her, that she was smiling ... and I knew that was a rarity.

After filling her in on my temporary Louisville locale, I told her how the label's powers-that-be were promoting me to a minimum wage position. It was a spectacular opportunity to continue to learn, grow, and actually make some money. Plus, I was getting a chance to cut a professional single. I could not have been more psyched.

"Congratulations! Wow. I knew it. It's gonna happen."

"We'll see," I said, not wanting to get my hopes up. After all, there were thousands of people who, like me, were searching for that same spotlight, which could only focus on a few select lucky individuals.

I think I heard Lara take in a breath before asking, "How's Audrey?"

"She had to stay in California for the holiday because she's low-person on the seniority list. I told her I'd stay, too, but she insisted I come home." Audrey had actually laughed at my protective offer, and I realized her independence was something I both admired and made me a little sad. I did like to make sure she was okay. "But she's good." I actually answered Lara's question. "Give her a wedding project and she forgets about everything else."

"Hmmm. Do you have a date set?"

"No. Waiting to get a little more settled." That was the suggestion from my parents. I was ready, but with everything else going on, it did make sense. "What about you? What are you up to, Miss Graduate? You're in Pittsburgh, right? How was your holiday?"

"Yeah and fine," she answered with a little less enthusiasm. "I've been job hunting, what else? It's hard. I'm sending out blind resumes and doing as much temp work as I can in the tech field. I just got one at a retirement home teaching the residents some of the latest technology."

"Oh God, that has to be an experience." I chuckled.

"Yeah, talk about starting from scratch. They already said they have to extend it so the senior citizens can understand the basics first. And by that, I mean power button!"

Fiddling with the personalized ornaments on our huge family Christmas tree, I told her what had immediately popped into my mind. "Those old guys are probably playing dumb because they all have crushes on you."

"Right, Finn." The exasperation in her voice said she didn't believe me at all.

"I know I'm right," I declared and wondered if she had started to grow her hair back out again.

No matter what, she was beautiful. She simply didn't see it. While I teetered on asking about her hair, the baby started wailing in the next room.

"You don't need to cry," Lara teased across the line. "I'll talk with you for a little while longer."

"Oh, you're a funny one. That's my nephew."

"Nephew? I didn't know you had a nephew. Your sister had the baby?"

See, I thought, there were so many things you miss telling someone when you aren't around them all the time. "Yep. He's a couple months old. It's my first time officially meeting him. That kid is a non-stop noisemaker!"

"I bet you love him to pieces though, huh?" She suddenly sounded kind of serene.

"Yeah. He's a keeper."

Wyatt was. He was such a cutie. And, as the first grandchild, he had everyone's hearts immediately.

"That's important," she replied in the same soft tone. "Your sister's happy?"

"Yeah. Yeah. The three of them are doing great."

"She's very lucky."

"I tell her that all the time. She really won the lottery when it came to getting me as a brother," I joked.

"Finn!" Lara admonished. "You know what I mean."

"I do. But it's fun to get that Lara reaction from you."

"Whatever." I couldn't see her, but I knew, without a shadow of a doubt, she was rolling her eyes. "I don't miss your teasing by the way."

"Yes, you do," I countered confidently.

"Okay," she admitted. "Maybe a little."

"Ditto." I acknowledged missing her and our easy-going banter. And then we talked about regular, everyday stuff for a little while before finally saying good-bye.

CHAPTER SEVENTEEN

Lara

The new year started similar to how the old one left off. The temp service kept me fairly busy doing odds-and-ends jobs, but they wouldn't last for long and, a lot of the time, the work was clerical. I needed something permanent and worthy of paying off my loans. So, I continued to send out resumes and went on some interviews but, otherwise, hibernated in the house, losing myself in novels or movies.

Part of the problem with getting a desirable job was that I focused on out-of-town positions. My feelings about staying in Western Pennsylvania hadn't faded. I still wanted out. I could feel how much my disposition had slipped into an almost depression since residing there again more permanently. My mom could see it, too, and as much as it wasn't because of her nor did she want me to move away, she understood.

So when I ended up getting a job in New York, it seemed ideal. It was miles and miles from home … in a whole new state. Plus, as the technology coordinator for a school, it perfectly matched my experience and interests.

"You're moving where? When?" Olivia's voice pitched

so high at the end that I was glad I had my phone on speaker or it may have hurt my ears.

"Soon."

I looked at the boxes I had already started packing. The job started in August, but I was moving out sooner. I had found an apartment online, and my mom and I had already made a trip to look it over in person and get things set financially. It was such a great feeling.

"New York?" Olivia questioned.

"Yeah," I confirmed.

"I totally would have never pictured you in the Big Apple."

Her shock made me wonder once again how people saw me. I don't think anyone had a clear or correct picture of the real Lara Faulkner. But, admittedly, I didn't let people in very easy … for due reason. And when I thought about it, I wasn't sure *I* even knew who I was. Maybe my next reinvention could be my true self … my final self … my happy self. I had started building a solid base for that foundation those couple of years in college, but I still needed to climb a few stories.

"It's not the city," I countered. "About an hour away … upstate. I'm sure I'll go into Manhattan, though. I always wanted to go there … see all the lights and people. Central Park, Times Square, the Empire State Building and—"

"We should do New Year's Eve!" Olivia exclaimed. "Yeah, that would be awesome."

I could picture Olivia and Sam smooching at the ball drop, and me standing there alone. Yeah … awesome. Not so much.

"Have you heard from Finn?"

"Well, that was a weird segue," she commented.

Yeah, I guess it was. Hmmm. "I was just thinking about how the four of us used to do things together. You were talking about meeting up in New York …"

"Yeah. Well, I wouldn't count the hillbilly in."

I rolled my eyes. Finn was far from a hillbilly. The ironic part was, Olivia's husband was more backwoods than any of us. The pig roast rehearsal dinner alone screamed that fact.

I let the thought go. "No. I know. California is too far. I haven't heard from him in a while, though," I commented on Finn's short and less frequent texts. "Just wondering if you guys have."

"No. Sam hasn't really either. He's probably, like, licking his wounds. What makes him think he will ever be some hotshot singer?"

"He *is* good, Liv." I defended one friend to another.

"Well, not so good that he shouldn't keep in touch with his friends."

She did kind of have a point. And while Olivia meant it in a derogatory sense, I thought about how Finn always was there for his friends. His trip to the hospital after the car accident, arriving at my dorm when my dad passed away, being in the wedding, and calling for my graduation was proof enough. Even if he did become a superstar, I didn't think he would change. It did make me wonder, though—was there something going on with Finn?

***

It took me a little while to get settled into my new place and job. Learning a new city, meeting new neighbors and colleagues, and understanding the curriculum needs were very time-consuming tasks. But once I did, I decided to try to get in touch with Finn. I emailed him an article about the movie we had gone to see the special preview for. It was getting the green light for yet another film in the series. The time we had gone to see the movie was one of my most favorite, carefree times with him, and the thought of reuniting somehow for the next film seemed so perfect. Maybe we could all find a way … whether it be in New York, West Virginia, or somewhere else.

When his email bounced back that it was no longer in use, I was immediately disheartened. I tried again—even typing it in from scratch and not relying on the automatic system— but it still didn't work, nor did it days later. Finn had obviously discontinued the service. Since I didn't have another address for him, I tried a text. I got the delivered message but might as well hadn't, since there was no reply … to that one or the follow-up I sent nearly a week later.

Finally, I gave up on typed correspondence and called directly. "Hey, it's, uh, Lara." I stumbled on my own name during the voice mail recording.

I was nervous, and I couldn't, at first, figure out why. It wasn't about any of those beyond-friendship feelings I had been struggling with. They were still there but getting tucked further away because of the reality of the situation. No. I realized the nerves were something even more internal. It was a strange feeling of finality. I knew Finn would get the message since his box wasn't full. And it seemed important to say the right thing because I felt like something was either wrong or coming to an end. It was weird … like Haylie and her silly supposed ESP.

"Hi," I tried to restart. "Where are you? I've texted, and I don't have your new email. I … I've moved. I want to tell you all about it. Totally not moseying along at the local mall." I smiled at my recall of our very first conversation in Sam's car. I hoped when he heard it, he would, too. "I want to hear all about you. I want to, you know, catch up." There was a lot more to say, but it felt weird leaving anything too personal on a recording and, besides, I really wanted to have an actual conversation. "Call me back, Finn. I … Yeah, call me back." As if somehow trying to channel him, I hung up the phone, turned on the local country music radio station, and waited for him to return the call.

But he didn't, and, admittedly, I was crushed. People who were important once weren't always going to be. That was another of those changes I should have been prepared for. Had I known when he called that past Christmas that it would have been the last time I would have heard his actual voice, I would have listened closer to the final words or made sure they were more relevant or meaningful. Or I simply would have said more.

Finn

I read Lara's texts. I saw her number come up on the screen as my phone rang. I heard the message she left. I did not reply to any.

At first it had been because of the super-speed everything was going at with my budding music career. But then ... then my world toppled and turned and twisted until I was so traumatized I couldn't even think straight.

A huge part of me wanted to reach out. I knew it might have even helped. It wouldn't have been right to bring her into my crazy world, though. I couldn't ... for her sake. It wouldn't have been fair.

CURRENT DAY

Finn

Album releases, bigger-than-ever concerts, award nominations … they were all huge deals and worthy of losing sleep over. Never had I ever tossed and turned as much as I did that night after I spoke with my sister, though. And it had nothing to do with the music business.

I couldn't get Lara out of my mind. After arriving back to my NYC penthouse, I had looked for any personal social media sites she might have. Alas, the search had been unsuccessful … just as it had been a couple years before and since I had known her. While it didn't surprise me, knowing how private she was, it *was* disappointing. So, without any luck, I had tried to go to sleep.

Flashbacks of our time together continued to swirl in my brain nonstop, though. It was our final two memories that kept me most awake—when I last saw her walking away at Sam and Olivia's wedding, and when we had last spoken on the phone for her graduation. I hadn't known, of course, that would be the last time. But it was. That had been my doing … my choice. It needed to be that way.

Now, though, it was different. It was years later, and *I*

was different. What would happen if I would actually see her again? I knew fate was definitely leading me in that direction, and, admittedly, I was both a little scared and a little excited about the prospect.

Having eventually found some kind of slumber, I woke the next morning a little later than usual. It was actually closer to when I would if it was the day following a concert on the road. After a shower and grabbing some coffee, I called my publicist, Reese.

"Already working on it," she answered, obviously recognizing my private number.

"What? What are you working on?"

"Whatever you think I should be," she answered with a laugh.

"Ha!" I legitimately chuckled. "I don't know, Reese. You always know before I know."

"That's how I keep my job."

There was some truth in her words. I couldn't ask for a better publicist. Her anticipation factor was top-notch. And she wouldn't let me forget that fact or let me get away with much. She was like having another older sister.

"If we get it confirmed today that your performance will open up the CMAs, I already have the copy ready for the releases."

"That would be awesome," I admitted. "I'm actually calling you about a much smaller venue, though." I glanced at the photo I found the night before. It was of Sam, Olivia, Lara, and me—just our hands layered on top of one another's.

"You are *not* going to play a kid's birthday party no matter how many mommy groups want it."

"No." God, no. "Although, it is about a kid."

I proceeded with telling Reese about my commitment to help Wyatt's school, but I didn't add any more details. She didn't need to know Lara's connection. My private life was just that … private. I guess I was like Lara in that way.

After hanging up, I tried to write some lyrics. My heart

was absolutely in the mood. Words like "home far away" and "country mountains" and "choices" and "chances" had my pencil dancing on the paper. But they were incomplete thoughts. I didn't know where to go with them besides feeling like there was something more. There had to be more. It was as if trying to choose when coming to a fork in the road.

Eventually, I gave in and set down the paper and my guitar. It was time, anyway, to make my way out of the energetic city and to Nola's house in the suburbs. Since I was leaving the next morning, the kids wanted to celebrate my impending September eleventh birthday while I was in town, and I couldn't think of a better way. Watching Wyatt and Kelsea smile was one of the best things in the world … even better than a chart-topping tune. Don't tell that to the powers-that-be, though.

***

When I got there, we had to wait for Will to return from work. In the meantime, Nola started setting out plates and napkins for the pizza. Wyatt and Kelsea were huddled in Wyatt's bedroom creating a special Uncle Finn birthday project. And I was checking my phone regarding my flight reservations back to Nashville.

"Geez, it's the landline," Nola called out from the kitchen when their home phone rang. "Who calls the landline?"

"Probably spam," I suggested. "I'll look. I'm next to it."

I stood up from the sofa and checked the caller ID on the phone's screen. When I read it was Wyatt's school, I almost bellowed the fact out to my sister. But then it hit me. It could be Lara. In fact, it probably was Lara. Nola had said my long-lost friend was going to call her to finalize things about me helping with the fundraiser.

The phone rang again, but most likely it was a third

time. My mind might have momentarily blipped to the past for a second or two again. Lara was just an answer away. She was right there if I picked up.

"Finn, who is it?" Nola questioned with a shout from the other room.

"It's the school." I ran my hands through my hair and along the side of my jeans. "I'll get it."

"Yeah," my sister agreed. "Might be a good idea."

"Hello?" I answered the phone and internally damned my voice for sounding so weird.

"Hi, uh, Mr. Jamison?" the caller on the other end asked.

Knowing that voice as if it was only a week and not years before when I had heard it last, I replied with the truth … but also anticipating her answer. "No. He's not here. Do you want to leave a message?"

"Who's this?" If I wasn't mistaken her voice sounded a little off that time, too.

"Hi, Lara. It's Finn."

~*~ ~*~ ~*~

What made Lara the way she was? Why did Finn stop talking with her? What happened with Audrey?

Want to read more of Lara and Finn's story? Be sure to pick up your copy of *Country Roads*! Reconnections will be made, revelations will be revealed, and a few tears will be shed.

A young woman content with her solitary life.

A rising country music star.

They were friends once ... until their lives took them down separate roads.

Now, years later, when a child volunteers his uncle to sing for a fundraiser, LARA FAULKNER realizes it is none other than her college pal, FINN MURPHY. As the two get a chance to reconnect, Lara reveals to a compassionate Finn details of her shocking past and the traumatic decision she had to make.

Through trust and love, the bond between Finn and Lara deepens as the country singer manages to get an emotionally scarred Lara to let down her self-proclaimed walls. But will secrets, lies, and tragedy cause a bumpy detour on their road to complete happiness?

Grab the whole series!

Available in Ebook and Print at all major book retailers.

ABOUT THE AUTHOR

There really wasn't any other path. Grea Warner knew from a young age that she wanted to write. She was born to write. First it was in diaries with little metal keys and in written tales that she slipped to friends in study hall. School newspapers, a college television drama, and the soap opera world were next. After producing and writing a local show, she decided to delve into the world of the novelist. When her fingers aren't tapping out her latest book filled with angst and romance, Grea can be found hiking the trails or jamming to her favorite country artists on the radio.

💻Website: http://greawarner.com/
💻Publisher   interview:
http://www.inkspellpublishing.com/grea-w...

✦Socials:
    Twitter: @grea_warner
    Instagram: greawarner
    Facebook: https://www.facebook.com/Grea-Warner
    YouTube   trailer   link:
https://www.youtube.com/watch?v=yrz9DjROoIM
    GoodReads:
https://www.goodreads.com/author/show/17230140.Grea_Warner
    BookBub: https://www.bookbub.com/authors/grea-warner